Just One Spark

THE BILLIONAIRE BARONS OF TEXAS ~ BOOK TWO

CHRIS KENISTON

Indie House Publishing

Indie House Publishing

MORE BOOKS

By Chris Keniston

The Billionaire Barons of Texas

Just One Date
Just One Spark
Just One Dance
Just One Take
Just One Taste
Just One Shot
Just One Chance

Hart Land

Heather
Lily
Violet
Iris
Hyacinth
Rose
Calytrix
Zinnia
Poppy
Picture Perfect

Farraday Country

Adam
Brooks
Connor
Declan
Ethan
Finn
Grace
Hannah
Ian
Jamison

Keeping Eileen
Loving Chloe
Morgan
Neil

Honeymoon Series

Honeymoon for One
Honeymoon for Three
Honeymoon for Four
Honeymoon for Five

Aloha Romance Series:

Aloha Texas
Almost Paradise
Mai Tai Marriage
Dive Into You
Look of Love
Love by Design
Love Walks In
Shell Game
Flirting with Paradise

Surf's Up Flirts:
(Aloha Series Companions)

Shall We Dance
Love on Tap
Head Over Heels
Perfect Match
Just One Kiss
It Had to Be You
Cat's Meow

ACKNOWLEDGMENT

Anyone who has read most of my books, and taken the time to read the acknowledgments as well, knows that without the help of a great many friends, these stories simply wouldn't happen.

For Kyle Baron's story so many things were outside my skill set. The entire idea of a race car driver hero meant that I had to find people who knew what side was up – so to speak lol. For this I must thank AJ and Courtney Garza. Not only for sharing their vast experience and understanding of racing including photos and videos to match, but for letting me get my baby snuggles in too. Y'all rock!

In order to write the sailing scene, I had to go all the way back to high school. Well, I didn't have to travel in time, but I did seek out a high school classmate. Colleen Talay and her husband Steve set me straight on terminology like mooring and heeling and a slew of other things that I hope helps every reader enjoy that feeling of gliding on water with the wind in your hair and a smile on your face. Without them, the racicng scene would never have come to life. Thank you Colleen!

As you may guess, I have on my own accord little knowledge of Go Karts, but I also am blessed to have a dear friend Michelle Jordan in the business. Her patience answering all sorts of questions and sharing unlimited photos and the use of her brother-in-law's name was immense. I would never have come up with the Quinceañera on my own! You're the best!

If there are any mistakes, know that they are all mine and not the fault of these generous friends!

Enjoy your visit with the Barons of Texas!

CHAPTER ONE

"**A**re you trying to give me a heart attack?" Kyle Baron's sister Eve threw her purse onto the white leather sofa on the family yacht and stood with her hands on her hips. "Do you have any idea how many years you just shaved off of my life?"

With only one hand, Kyle poured himself a drink.

Eve glared at her brother. "A little early in the day to start drinking, don't you think?"

"It would be if it were something stronger than cola." He took a slow sip of the fizzing drink. "I gather Gilbert called you?"

"He. Did."

The sharpness in his sister's voice made the hackles on the back of his neck rise. He did his best not to wince at the venomous tone. "Do I want to know what he said?"

Her hands still fisted firmly on her hips, she stared daggers at him. "I was informed, in a voice mail, that you went skydiving. That alone wasn't alarming considering speed and risk go hand and hand with you. We're all used to it. The problem is the next part. Apparently, you had a *little* accident."

He didn't dare meet her gaze.

"How the hell do you have a *little* accident falling thousands of feet out of an airplane?"

"You don't."

"Exactly." Now her foot was tapping. "I had visions of your body splattered across miles of empty field. Piece by bloody piece."

Now he did wince.

"Thank heavens the hospital informed me you were

alive before I called Mom or worse, the Governor and Grams. News like you'd been in a skydiving accident could have sent all three of them to their graves. At least all I need now is for my hairdresser to hide the newly sprouted strands of gray."

He really would have to have a chat with Gilbert about what information his manager shared with his next of kin. In Kyle's profession, there just might be a day when he really was sprawled piece by piece across a track and voice mail was not how he wanted his family told. "I'm sorry. Really."

Finally, on a long slow breath, her hands fell to her sides and a softer expression washed over her face. "Why couldn't you have been an accountant?"

That made him chuckle. His entire life his mother had tried to steer him in the direction of a stable career. What she really meant was safe. Sadly for his mother's nerves, few things in life could beat the adrenaline rush of coming across the finish line at almost 200 mph. If there was a thrill involved, whether it was on land, on the water, or in the air, Kyle was all in. To his family's chagrin, he'd opted for a high-risk land career. More precisely, racing. Precious little beat flying around a track and leaving others in your dust. The only career possibly more invigorating than racing might have been a fighter pilot. Both machines were powerful, required skilled operators with nerves of steel to maneuver, and provided the opportunity for speed on steroids. Even though there wasn't a doubt in anyone's mind that Kyle was an adrenaline junkie who had the right stuff to be a jet jock, having grown up in the limelight of a former Marine Lieutenant Colonel, Kyle knew following strict orders twenty-four seven was not his thing. He needed freedom and control to do what he wanted when he wanted.

Which is how he wound up here now with a very distraught sister. Still feeling the need for some of that in-flight adrenaline, skydiving was his ticket. What he hadn't expected was for the statistics on his way of life to kick in now. Too many drivers fell into adversity not on the track as spectators would expect, but after the races. As with drivers who survived long careers behind the wheel unscathed only to be taken out skiing or cleaning gutters, he'd enjoyed an injury free career so far only to find himself in a cast for the next six weeks, not from a racetrack mishap, not even from his recent tumble out of an airplane. No, his broken wrist came from slipping on a bar of soap while changing in the men's room after successfully skydiving on a clear sunny day.

"How long are you out for?"

Lost in his own thoughts about the stupid fall, the extra challenges his absence from the circuit would mean for his team and the green back up driver, he struggled for the words to make his sister feel at least a little better. "Maybe six weeks."

"Maybe?" One brow rose higher than the other, and shaking her head, she blew out a sigh and stood up. "I think I need that drink."

"Isn't it a little early in the day," he teased.

"It's five o'clock somewhere."

Kyle followed his sister to the bar and too quickly realized with only one working hand, he was not going to be uncorking wine bottles anytime soon. At least the injury had happened during the summer break—one of the reason's he'd gone skydiving at all. With three weeks left to the natural hiatus, he'd only miss one or two season races at best.

"So." She poured half a glass of her favorite white merlot. "What's the plan?"

"Plan?"

"Yes. You're injured. Last time I looked, even if you could work the paddle shifters, there's no way to undo your harness and remove the steering wheel fast enough to qualify for the race with one hand in a cast."

Didn't he know that one. It also didn't help any that the darn wrist was throbbing despite the meds the doctor had given him. "No driving for now."

"And jumping out of airplanes? Or do you need two hands for that?"

"One hand will do, but I'm not planning on going back

out anytime soon."

"Well, there's that." She took a slow sip of her wine. "At least none of us will have to worry for a little while."

And that darn near broke his heart. As much as he loved racing for a living, he hated worrying his family. "I really am sorry Gilbert scared you."

"I know." For the first time since she'd stomped onto the yacht, the corners of her mouth tipped upward in a tired smile. She leaned in and kissed his cheek. "I have an idea."

"Should I be worried?" Sometimes his brilliant geeky sister came up with fantastic ideas, and other times, well, he and his brothers were better off running for the hills.

She rolled her eyes skyward. "Since you can't try and kill yourself for the next few weeks, why don't you recuperate at the ranch? Grams would love to have you and I think having you intact under her roof will make this little accident more palatable."

His kid sister had a point. At least this idea wouldn't be so awful. As a matter of fact, it was a pretty good idea. He loved the ranch as much as the yacht, but moored off shore, the Baroness could start to feel stifling, especially for six weeks. Yep, bless his little sister, she was right, the ranch and his grandmother's love was just what the doctor ordered.

Addison Raymond stared at the screen in front of her, shook her head, and then picking up a traditional number two pencil, began scribbling on a scratch pad.

"I don't know how you use those things." Her coworker Jen stood in the entryway of the oversized cubicle that didn't quite qualify as a private office.

"You know I don't like mechanical pencils." Even as a little kid, she loved drawing with sharpened pencils. To her, mechanical pencils always felt dull. There was also something soothing about the whirring sound of an electric pencil sharpener.

"You also may be the only person in the building who actually sharpens pencils."

"That's not possible." There were plenty of old fogies in her department who still used pencils, adding machines, and white board. Though in all honesty, she had no idea why those same people had a deep rooted aversion to software. Still struggling with her latest project, she tossed the pencil down, leaned back in the chair and smiled up at her friend. "Can I help with anything?"

Jen shook her head. "Not unless you know someone looking for a mechanical engineer who hasn't done engineering in a very long while."

"What? Why?"

"Deb in personnel just told me on the QT that an emergency board meeting was called this morning."

Addison glanced down the hall. She couldn't see the executive board room from her space, but she had noticed the CEO and a few other company bigwigs getting off the elevator a couple of hours ago. "Are we sure it's not a scheduled meeting? You know how the good old boys love an excuse to show off to each other."

"I wish. Rumor is that the quarterly reports are in and are disastrous. Next quarter's forecast isn't any better."

"This won't be the first time the numbers have been bad. We've weathered economic downturns before and survived."

Jen spun around and leaned back on the desk. "This time feels different. Electric cars and green energy weren't as popular as they are now."

"Or as politically correct." As much as she wished it weren't so, there was a knot in her stomach that had been twisting every so often with the negative news reports and industry gossip. "Let's just hope the grapevine has got it all wrong."

"I hope so."

As difficult as it was, Addison did her best to paste on a reassuring smile. "Like I said, we've weathered worse."

"From your mouth to God's ears." Jen pushed away from the desk. "I'd better get back to my cubby. Just in case you're right and I really do still have a job."

"There you go," Addison chuckled, "positive attitude."

Jen rolled her eyes and raising one finger in the air in an off handed wave, continued down the hall.

Reaching for her freshly sharpened pencil, Addison returned to the challenges at hand. She knew the answer was right in front of her and she simply wasn't seeing it. Maybe it was time for a little fresh air. Clean her mental pallet. Between her cubicle here in town and her office at home, she spent too much time hovered over a desk. She really did need to stop taking her work home with her. Spend more down time with friends. Catch a movie in a real theater with real surround sound. She didn't dare stop to reflect on how long had it been since she'd spent an hour with anyone who wasn't on the company payroll.

As soon as this project was finalized, she'd do that. She would, but for now, water bottle in hand, she strolled down the hall and pushed the elevator button. One of the things she loved about working in downtown Houston this time of year was access to the rooftop patio. A few minutes high above the world might give her new perspective.

The door behind her opened and one by one, the company executives filed out of the board room. Low murmurs filled the narrow hallway slowly ebbing to unnatural silence. The elevator door opened and she was tempted to lag behind in case anyone actually said anything important, hopefully reassuring. Instead, she went about her business. After all, that's what she was getting paid for, not for eavesdropping.

Three of the dozen execs stepped into the elevator with her. The silence hung heavily. Using the special key for the senior executive floor, the three others exited the small space in continued silence. The ropes that had twisted on and off in her stomach recently, now weighed heavily inside her. Like it or not, her gut screamed Jen was right. Something very unpleasant just went down in that all-morning meeting and if in the end she wasn't looking for a new job, then her name wasn't Addison Lynn Ray.

CHAPTER TWO

"Yes." Even though his brother couldn't see him, Kyle bobbed his head. "I get it. It won't happen again."

"Isn't it bad enough that every time you climb behind the wheel of that bazillion dollar car, we all have to hold our breaths until the race is over?" Of all his brothers, Craig had been the most understanding about Kyle's career choice. Except maybe today.

"I said I get it."

"Do you? Do you really? What part of your brain considered that jumping out of an airplane wouldn't shave ten years off of Gram's life?"

He didn't dare bring up the fact that he'd been jumping out of planes almost as long as he'd been driving a car. The troops were gathering, circling the wagons so to speak, and all to protect their grandmother, Lila. "Please keep in mind that thousands of civilians jump out of airplanes every day and live to tell about it." Now most likely was not the time to bring up that watching all the people coughing up good money to jump out of an airplane had him considering investing in a local skydiving operation. Heaven knew there was enough Baron land in South Central Texas for running one of the biggest herds in the state. With their own runway already on the property, how hard would it be to pick a spot and start collecting some of those eager tourists' money?

"Are you even listening?"

"Sorry. My mind wandered."

"How you manage to focus behind the wheel of those cars you race is beyond me." Exasperation dripped from Craig's every word. "What time will you be at the house?"

"I'm almost there. Another thirty minutes and you can yell at me in person."

There was a long silent moment, the first one that Craig had let pass between them. "Are you supposed to be driving with that arm?"

"I'm in Eve's car. We swapped." His sister was an excellent driver and fully capable of handling a stick shift, but preferred the comfort of a luxury automatic.

"You let Eve drive the Aston?" The sound of exasperation was now replaced with deserved incredulity.

Kyle never let anyone drive his baby, until now. "Don't remind me."

"Oh, man. Are you sure you didn't hit your head too?"

"Hardy har har. My head is fine, thank you very much." Ahead on the two lane road that led to Baron land, a small car seemed to be eking along. That was the only downside to country roads and city drivers. Locals could take the curves at a respectable speed as long as there weren't any cows loose on the roads. All he wanted was to get to the ranch, breathe in fresh air, and drink some of Hazel's fresh lemonade. Maybe down a few aspirins with it. That is, if the slow poke ahead ever found the gas pedal on the right.

Lord knows what people did on road trips before GPS. Several miles back Addison's phone had lit up with a detour. She'd almost ignored it, and then, when she veered off the exit just as the cars ahead began to flash red tail lights, she was glad she'd followed the altered directions. From the side road she was on she could see the freeway not far beside her and the northbound parking lot it had become. If she hadn't turned off, she'd be sitting in that for who knew how long.

Even bypassing the traffic, the little detour was going to get her to her mom's twenty minutes later than expected. Which was considerably better than hours. For a lousy twenty minutes she wasn't going to bother calling her mother, especially since any number of additional delays and detours could pop up in the next couple of hours. At least the view from up here was much nicer than the freeway. She always knew there was plenty of cow country between Houston and North Texas, and from time to time caught glimpses of cattle or horses grazing along the sides of the freeway, but from this road she had a wonderful view of the rolling hill-scape to the west of the freeway. The whole thing made her wonder how much more did the state have to offer that she never got to see.

What she didn't see anywhere was a house. Not a single one. Surely someone had to live out this way. Suddenly she was really glad she got an early start. She couldn't imagine maneuvering these narrow roads out in the middle of nowhere in the dark. Always keeping an eye in the rearview mirror, she was surprised to see a spot in the distance gaining on her, quickly. "Idiot must be flying."

It was the same thing on the freeway. Every so often some speedster would fly past everyone at twenty or more miles over the speed limit. Like saving ten minutes was going to make their lives any better.

The car in the distance was closing the gap. The one thing these old country roads were missing was the breakdown lane. A narrow strip of dirt, grass, or gravel was on either side of the road, but not enough room for her to pull over. She tried picking up the speed a little, but with all the curves, she wasn't comfortable going much faster than she was, and she had no doubt that a little faster wasn't going to make any difference. The guy was growing exponentially closer and her grip was tightening on the steering wheel almost as quickly.

At least the man had some manners. With only the two of them on the road, the driver actually signaled he was moving left. Since there was no left lane, only a single lane in each direction, she could only assume his intention was to pass her. Good riddance. Bracing herself, she kept her gaze mostly on the rearview mirror. The car was coming so close she could finally make out the color, and she was pretty sure that was a Mercedes logo on the hood. Great.

Fast, stupid *and* rich. What a combination.

Maybe if she slowed down just a little, he'd pass her even sooner. Yes. She needed this guy off her rear-end before he wound up sitting, engine and all, in her backseat. Easing her foot off the gas pedal, she sucked in a deep calming breath and tearing her gaze away from the rearview mirror, stared at the road in front of her. Nearly at the top of the low hill, she returned her attention to the car now close enough to kiss her trunk.

Relief slowly gurgled to the forefront as the car shifted left into the other lane. A couple more minutes and it would all be over and she could go back to enjoying the scenery. At the crest of the hill, she kept her eyes on the road, the blacktop, the solid yellow line between the two lanes, and, oh dear lord, the huge truck coming their way!

"Oh, sh—" Kyle dropped the phone and did a hard pull on the steering wheel. The Mercedes did not handle like his Aston and he wished to heck he had two good arms and a stick shift. All he could do was hit the gas and pray he didn't lose control. When the truck skirted by within inches and continued on his merry way, Kyle actually wondered if he wasn't running out of lives.

A quick glance in the rearview mirror and where the heck had the car… "Oh, crud." The small car he'd tried to pass was nowhere in sight, but a huge dust cloud where it should have been was now blowing behind him. "Blast."

Doing a fast one eighty u-turn, he hit the gas as hard as he dared and flew down the few yards to where the car should have been. This was not looking so good. And worse, his brother was on the other end of the phone. Kyle could hear Craig's muffled voice yelling for him. There was no time to go fishing for a phone. "There's been a little incident," he spoke into the empty car. "I'll call you back in a few." He really hoped his brother could hear him. If he continued to use other cars during his stay he needed to remember to connect his phone to the dashboard. This talking as you drive with the phone in your lap was for the birds.

Screeching to a halt by the cloud of dust, he hopped out of his car as fast as he could and wished Mercedes made cars without doors like his racecars. Feet on the ground, he ran at a full gallop. Only some of the cloud was dust, the rest was smoke. "Crap."

Thankful he'd only hurt his arm and not his legs, he reached the car and blew out a sigh of relief as the driver side door inched open. Grabbing hold of the handle with his good arm, he pulled it open all the way.

Big brown eyes under long lush lashes squinted up at him. "What the hell were you thinking?"

"I wasn't." He extended his uninjured hand to her. "Are you okay? Hurt anywhere?"

One foot out the door, she stopped as though she hadn't previously taken stock of whether or not she was okay.

"Need some help?" His hand remained extended in front of her.

A thoughtful gaze narrowed under buckled brows as her hand swatted his. "Thank you, you've done enough."

At least she didn't sound like she had a concussion. Of course in the real world that didn't matter much. "Don't move too quickly. Are you sure nothing's hurt?"

Those big brown eyes turned almost black as her lips pressed tightly together and with one good effort she pushed to her feet. "I'm fine." Spinning about to look at the car behind her, her shoulders immediately slumped. "Not so much my car."

Still studying her for any signs of dizziness, imbalance, bruising, nausea, convinced that on the surface she was fine, he tore his gaze away to examine the car. Except for the sturdy pecan tree that had stopped her slide and wedged itself in the front passenger bumper, the car was actually in pretty good shape. "Will it start?"

"What?" Now her forehead pleated and she looked at him as if he'd spoken to her in ancient Phoenician.

"Will the engine turn on?"

"I don't see where it matters with that tree growing out of my front tire."

"Please?"

On a huff, she sat back down and gripped the keys. "If I blow us up, you get to explain to my mother that it's all your fault."

He bit back a smile and nodded. "Deal."

Slowly, she turned the key and the engine roared to life.

"Good." He flashed his most winsome smile, the one that usually got him anything he wanted, but from her deep-set frown, it clearly wasn't working on her. "Give me a minute, please."

He trotted back to Eve's car and grabbed his phone from the floorboard. Hurrying to the woman's side, he hit speed dial on his phone and waited for the other end to answer.

"Are you calling 911?"

He shook his head. "My grandfather."

"Shouldn't we call the police?" The frown was growing deeper as she turned to her car.

"Sir. We have a little incident."

"Not again. Break the other arm?" the gruff voice carried from the speaker phone.

"My other arm is fine, but please have Mack send a tow truck. There's been an accident and we need to fix a fender and probably a tire."

"Eve's car?"

"No." Shaking his head as if his grandfather could see him, he dropped the phone to his side. "I'm sorry, what's your name?"

"Addison."

"Nice to meet you. I'm Kyle." He didn't wait for her response before lifting the phone to his ear again. "Addison went off the road. We're about five miles south of the main gate. Send Mack." He slid the phone into his pocket and put on his best smile, again. "So, Addison. What brings you to this lonely road?"

CHAPTER THREE

How she let this stranger talk her into joining him for lunch, she had no idea. One minute Addison was standing by the car, flustered after having been practically pushed off the road by the speeding lunatic. The next thing she knew there was a tall good looking cowboy and a bow-legged old guy pulling up, neither of which seemed any happier with the driver than she was. And now, here she was riding on the passenger side of the sleek Mercedes.

"My brother can be a bit overbearing, but he's really a pussycat."

That wasn't the first word that came to mind. The two brothers were about the same height with wavy chestnut hair cut just above the collar. Neat, but not boring. Just enough hair for a girl to run her fingers through. Not that she had any intention of running her fingers through Kyle or his brother's hair any time soon—or ever.

It hadn't taken long to leave the quiet country roads behind and find herself coming down what she suspected was a main drag for this part of the county. Having grown up in a somewhat rural area of North Texas, the idea of small town wasn't new to Addison, but nonetheless, this small of a small town was a bit out of her element.

"I'm afraid there isn't very much close by in terms of food options, but Willa's Café is clean, roomy, and the home cooking has been keeping neighbors coming back for as long as I can remember." The Mercedes turned into the parking lot just on the other side of the northbound freeway.

"Maybe," she gripped her seatbelt without unlatching it, "we should just go to the mechanic and see what he says about my car."

Kyle shook his head and pulled into an empty spot directly in front of the double doors. "We've been over this. It's not a five minute fix and there isn't anything we could do standing around watching Mack and his boys work."

Yes. They had discussed this. Even the brother who was less than happy with Kyle had agreed there was nothing they could do except wait and they might as well wait over a good meal. Except she wasn't hungry. Her stomach was still twisting and discontent. When the dust settled from the unexpected board meeting the other day, she'd not been terribly surprised to discover Jen had been correct. The hatchet had fallen not only on Jennifer and Addison, but on half of their department. At least the boom came with a nice severance check and excellent references. Both of which bought her a little bit of time to figure out her next move, find a new job—and accept that maybe it was time to get out of the volatile oil and gas business. In the meantime, she was supposed to have a relaxing nice long visit with her mother. How long depended on her job search and whether they got on each other's nerves the way mothers and daughters often do. Hopefully today's incident was not going to be indicative of the rest of her stay.

"Well, isn't this a nice surprise," a heavyset man in a white apron called out from the window open to the kitchen.

Kyle smiled and waved at the gentleman. "Hey, Fred. Always make it a point to stop by when I can. What do you say looks good for today?" His good hand at her lower back, Kyle nudged Addison toward the archway to a large dining area.

"Everything is good."

"Always is." Kyle's grin broadened.

"But you might want to try Mamma's brisket pie. Just sayin'."

"Brisket pie?" Addison almost whispered at him.

"Shepherd's pie made with smoked brisket instead of ground beef. One of Willa's famous recipes."

"Ah." She nodded and followed his lead across the large dining room.

The sound of wooden chairs scraping along the tile floor reverberated in the large space as a big beefy guy pushed to his feet and extended his hand mid air in Kyle's direction. "I heard you'd be missing a few weeks of the circuit. Spending it with the Governor?"

Governor? Addison felt a need to stand a little straighter. Surely they didn't mean the actual Texas governor.

Kyle nodded his head. "Can't miss a chance to spend time with Grams and the Governor."

For just a second she wondered if maybe Kyle's grandfather was British and Governor was just a nickname. Like Bert had called Mr. Banks in the Mary Poppins movie? After all, the current governor of Texas wasn't old enough to be Kyle's grandfather.

The two men chatted for a few minutes about things she didn't quite follow. It took a few more minutes to make it to the corner table stopping every few feet to say hello to one local or another, all of who felt compelled to bring up his unexpected visit, his absence from the circuit—whatever that meant—and his bum arm. She kept waiting for someone to say something more about the circuit for her to figure it out, but apparently everyone in the place knew him and had no interest in explaining themselves for her benefit.

By the time they were finally settled at the table, a steady flow of people had stopped to say hello. Most seemed genuinely surprised and happy to see him, so much so that she felt like she'd stopped to lunch with the prodigal son.

"You seem pretty popular." She drew the paper napkin from the table and spread it across her lap.

"It's a small town. Everyone knows everybody." He reached for the single page menu stacked at the edge of the table. "Growing up, my siblings, cousins and I spent as much time on my grandparents' ranch during the summers as we did in our own homes. Now that we're all grown, we don't spend near as much time as we should, or would like to, and certainly don't see many of the townsfolk anymore. When we do bump into people, they're usually happy to see us."

"I see." She glanced at the menu and tried to sneak a peek at the man perusing the single piece of paper. There was no reason to doubt what he'd just said about small towns knowing everyone. Heaven knew the concept certainly was real where she had grown up, but still, she had this feeling there was more to the story than a simple case of neighbors having their nose in everyone's business. Or maybe her imagination was simply working overtime.

Kyle had thought for sure that anyone else would have put two and two together by now and figured out that he was not only a Baron, but a somewhat popular with the media Baron. From what he could see, Addison truly had no idea who he was. "See something you like?"

"I see a lot of things I wouldn't mind trying, but that brisket pie has piqued my interest."

"It's delicious."

"Sounds like everything is."

"What do you like to eat?"

"Anything with meat. I'm a carnivore through and through."

That made Kyle chuckle. Not many women were willing to admit they'd prefer a good steak to a heart healthy salad. "You never did tell me."

Her head tipped to one side, she lifted her gaze to meet his. "Tell you what?"

"What brought you to the country road we, uh, met on."

"Met." She smothered a laugh. "That's one way to put it."

She had a lovely smile. He was glad to get the chance to see it. Considering how upset she was, and rightfully so, after having been run off the road, and how stiff she was in the short ride to the café, he was almost surprised to see her so relaxed and smiling. "So, what brings you to these parts?"

"On my way to my mother's for a short visit."

"You don't live around here." He set his menu down. He hadn't actually needed to see what was available. Anyone from these parts knew the menu by heart and in this case, as soon as Fred had suggested the brisket pie, he'd known what he was going to eat.

She shook her head. "We're about half way between my mothers and where I live outside of Houston. At least for now."

"For now?"

A deep sigh escaped her lips and for the first time since running her off the road, he got the impression that more was wrong with Addison's world than his impatient driving. Her gaze fell to the silverware at her fingertips. "I'm thinking of making some changes."

He almost asked what kind of changes, but then decided that keeping quiet and letting her talk would probably give him more answers.

"It seems I have been blessed with an unexpected vacation."

In other words, she just lost her job. "What is it you do?"

"Mechanical engineer."

Impressive. Perhaps a little chauvinistic of him, but that wasn't the answer he had expected. Putting two and two together, it was easy to draw conclusions. "Oil and gas?"

She nodded.

He didn't have to be a genius to know the volatility of that particular industry. The Houston skyline was peppered with large and small companies who had made and lost fortunes in the oil business. He was sorely tempted to ask why she had lost her job, but it really was none of his business.

At that moment, a gum snapping waitress he didn't recognize came to a stop at their table and set two glasses of water in front of them. "Do you know what you'd like? Or do you need more time?"

He dipped his chin in Addison's direction. "Ready?"

"Yes. I'll have the brisket pie. House salad, blue cheese dressing on the side."

"I'll have the same."

"Got it. I'll have that out shortly."

He waited until the young server was out of earshot. "Do you have any interim plans?"

A sincere smile took over her face. "I do. Growing up, I spent a lot of time at the local animal shelter. There's always a need for volunteers. I love my mother, but hanging out 24/7 isn't always the best idea. I thought I would help out at the shelter until I decide what to do next."

He didn't need to know the circumstances of losing her job, he considered himself an excellent judge of character, and the little he'd learned about Addison told him she had more than her share of character. "Admirable."

Hefting one shoulder in a lazy shrug, she continued to smile at him. A very nice smile. "Not that admirable. I love being around animals. Of course, the only problem is that I want to bring them all home."

"I gather that didn't go over well with your folks."

"My dad died when I was a little girl, and while my mom didn't mind when I brought home a German Shepherd puppy who needed to be bottle fed, she put her foot down the first time I came home with a boxful of kittens."

"Oh, I bet." He didn't want to think how his mother would have reacted. Though there were plenty of animals at the ranch, their Houston home was just big enough for the five kids growing up and one dog. Anything more and his mom would have gone apoplectic. Though there was one thing he felt confident that his mother wouldn't have objected to. Bringing home a nice girl like Addison Ray. Even if she was unemployed. "Do you have any more long term plans?"

She shook her head. "At this point I figure a week to decompress, hang out with Mom, and play with the shelter animals will hopefully give me some perspective."

Now was probably not the time to kick in his two cents and mention that perspective could be grossly over rated. Of course that didn't say much coming from someone who had known his entire life that he wanted to play for a living.

Since fixing her car wasn't going to be as easy as

undoing a loose screw, they took their time chatting over lunch. In some ways, she reminded him of his sister. Smart, competent—even if her bosses weren't current on that part—and a tendency to shift into quiet mode. He was sorely tempted to invite her to dinner. A real dinner with fabric napkins and a French chef. But his nice girl radar had sounded long before she set foot in his car and giving her back her repaired car and sending her on her merry way was definitely the smart thing to do. Then again, a few of his siblings might argue that he wasn't necessarily the sharpest knife in the drawer.

CHAPTER FOUR

"You're up nice and early this morning." Sitting at one end of the breakfast table, Kyle's grandmother smiled sweetly and tipped her cheek in his direction in anticipation of a kiss.

As kids they would often line up for their grandmother's hugs and kisses. She had a way of making each of them feel as if they were her favorite grandchild without coming right out and saying so. Just being in the same room with her still made Kyle feel like that safe and content little kid basking in the love the older woman eagerly bestowed on them. As far as he was concerned, his grandmother was a living, breathing testament to unconditional love.

"Hazel made blueberry pancakes this morning."

His favorite. Not that out of box fare, but completely from scratch, light as a feather, and exceptionally delicious breakfast food. "Sounds wonderful."

"You know she made them just for you." Eve smiled up at him. Ever since his business manager had called her to inform her that her reckless brother had jumped out of an airplane and broken his wrist in a different fall, she'd opted to stay at the family ranch too. Most likely to make sure he didn't do anything stupid to really kill himself. Completely over-protective and he loved her to death for it.

"Good morning." Craig looked up from the seat beside their sister. "Didn't expect to see you this early in the day."

How early was it? He flipped his good wrist and looked at his new fangled watch that reported everything short of his blood type.

"Mitch and Devlin are down at the stables." Dressed in

jeans and a plain cotton button down shirt, his brother Craig was clearly dressed to join them. "A couple of the hands have come down with a bug so we told the Governor we'd chip in today."

Kyle nodded. "Let me shovel down some of those pancakes, not to hurt Hazel's feelings of course."

"Of course." Eve chuckled softly.

"Then I'll come down and join you." He reached for the silver coffee pot.

"Not necessary." Craig shook his head. "We've got this covered and you're short one good arm."

"Can still do a lot with the other."

Eve stretched her arm out and patted his hand. "It's okay to take it easy for a bit longer. The others can handle it."

The look in her eyes stabbed at him. When he was behind the wheel of what he considered to be an extremely safe car, the last thing he thought about was what his family was going through watching him from the stands or on TV from the comfort of their living rooms. If every time he ran a race, this image was in his mind, he might have wound up in a different career. "Love you."

The rhythmic tapping of his grandfather's cane sounded from down the hall, his instructions to Jeeves reaching them seconds before the old man walked through the doorway. "It's good to have so many of the boys working together again."

Grams smiled up at her longtime husband. "Chase called and if he and CJ can get away early they'll come today to help, otherwise they'll be here for Sunday dinner tomorrow."

The Governor nodded. His expression was mostly blank, but those who knew him well would recognize the pleased glint in his eyes. Practically from the first moment he'd met CJ almost a year ago, the Governor had taken a shine to the former Marine nurse, even though to this day the old man had no idea Chase had tried to pull the wool over his eyes. Giving his wife a guarded peck on the cheek and a quick squeeze of her hand, his grandfather took a seat at the opposite end of the long table. "Another calf was rejected."

"Oh, how sad." Lila Baron set her porcelain teacup into the saucer. "I wonder why so many this year?"

"Mother Nature can be fickle." The Governor poured steaming coffee into a large mug with Semper Fi emblazoned on both sides. "If Mitch hadn't gone into politics he'd make a great rancher."

Lila nodded. "He is the sensitive one."

"Didn't take him long at all to get another one of the cows who lost her own to take this one on as if it were hers. Mitch just has the touch."

"That he does." Their grandmother took a slow sip of her tea.

"So," the Governor reached for a croissant, "how is the wrist doing?"

Considering it had been less than a week since Kyle went skating across the bathroom floor, not much different than when his grandfather had asked him about it upon his arrival a few days ago. "Getting better."

"Hm," the old man grunted.

"I think I'm going to head to the stable and check on those new calves." Eve dabbed at the corners of her mouth with her napkin and pushed away from the table. Dressed in jeans and her favorite pink boots, she looked just like any rancher and worlds apart from the fashion magazine worthy attire she normally wore.

"Make sure your brothers and cousin don't get into any trouble," Lila Baron teased her granddaughter.

"No worries there. I've been riding rough-shod over them most of my life."

"That's my girl." Her grandmother winked.

Their grandfather kept an eye on his granddaughter until she was out of sight. "It makes no sense."

"No, it doesn't, dear."

One of the many things that both fascinated and frustrated the younger generation of Barons was how the two elders always seemed to know what the other was talking about. Sometimes without words. Though this time, he had a good idea the conversation was the same old bone that had his brother Chase renting a date for his cousin Andrew's wedding. Anything to avoid their grandfather harping on their love lives, or more particularly, lack of marital bliss. Though they'd set the bar awfully high, the Governor and Grams were as much an inspiration as a deterrent. Attaining relationship perfection was not an easy thing for mere mortals.

"Perhaps," the Governor looked to Kyle, "this downtime could be an excellent opportunity to work on your personal life."

"My personal life is just fine, thank you."

"Solitary seems to be a more accurate description. I could invite the Kessler sisters to join us for dinner one night this week. It's been a long while since you've seen them."

And with the grace of God it would be a good long while before he had to see them again. "That won't be necessary, Governor."

The old man rolled his eyes.

This was not good. Memories of the Governor setting his brother up with Prudence Van Klein's boring wallflower of a daughter during one of Mitch's fundraisers came rushing to mind. "As a matter of fact," he cleared his throat, "I've met someone."

His grandfather's eyes opened wide. "Anyone we know?"

Kyle shook his head. He was walking a thin line of misdirection, but didn't want to outright lie. "I've only just met her myself. She's very nice. Smart too."

"Really?" That seemed to catch his grandfather's interest.

"An engineer. I think you'd like her." Not that his grandfather would ever meet her in person to find out. Especially since she took off the other day faster than the cartoon roadrunner once Mack delivered her car. All he knew about her was that she'd lost her job and her mother lived somewhere just south of Corsicana. And that she planned to volunteer at the animal shelter. *The animal shelter*. There was an idea.

"Isn't she a cutie." Addison held up one of the fluffy kittens that had been dropped off at the doorstep this morning in a cardboard box. "I don't understand how people can just abandon them."

"At least they abandoned them someplace where they'd be cared for. Nothing worse than the heartless jerks who dump faithful pets out in the woods alone and unable to fend for themselves." Maureen, one of the teenage summer volunteers, continued bathing the other kittens.

"I don't even want to think about those. Breaks my heart."

"You ever consider becoming a foster for some of these guys who can't find homes?"

"I wish, but I'd be an epic failure and wind up with an apartment full of animals. Take crazy cat lady to a whole new level."

"Maybe you can talk your mother into taking one or two. How big is her yard?"

"Not that big." Addison laughed. "Maybe we could talk her into one little dog. Very little."

The teen chuckled with her, then looking up at one of the monitors for the exterior cameras whistled. "Ooh. Looks like we've got a live one." She set the damp kitten down on a towel. "Can you dry them off?"

Addison nodded.

"Good. I'll be right back."

Toweling the little ones, she saw the bright red two door car that had caught the kid's attention. She had no idea what brand it was, but there was no doubt whatever it was it was very expensive. Hopefully the owner was here to adopt one of the older pets that few people were interested in. Wouldn't that be nice.

One kitten wrapped in a small towel, she glanced up at the monitors that showed different viewpoints of the outside and lobby of the small shelter. The man who climbed out of the sports car stood tall and straight. Like half the men in

Texas cattle country, he wore the standard uniform of jeans, boots, and a wide brimmed Stetson. It took a couple more minutes of drying kittens and glancing up at the monitors before she recognized the stealth strut of the stranger. At least she thought she recognized him. Or maybe it was just wishful thinking.

The longer she and Kyle sat eating lunch the other day, the easier the conversation had gotten. By the time the mechanic returned with her car, she was good and rightly smitten with the man who seemed to be nothing like the hotheaded speedster she'd thought him to be when he accidentally ran her off the road. Though she'd decided he was at least a little bit of a nice guy when he turned around to check on her. And it wasn't totally his fault that he had to swerve to avoid the truck. Of course there was no excuse for trying to pass her on a blind hill, but no one was perfect. Flipping the switch on the dashboard, she turned on the speakers and listened in to the conversation.

"Welcome to the Happy Paws Shelter," Maureen said through a silver-coated smile. The braces might have exaggerated her youth, but the kid had volunteered enough years to be the shelter's best advocate. If anyone could talk a tough-skinned bachelor into a pet, she could.

"Thank you." He casually glanced around, looking over her shoulder, then back to the small open pens set up in the lobby to soft sell adoptions to all folks who entered, whether that was their intent or not. His gaze seemed to linger a moment longer on the pen with a couple of border collie mixed pups and an oversized mutt who had taken to mothering them.

"They're adorable, aren't they?" Maureen hurried over to the pen and immediately lifted the runt into her arms. "We try not to name them, but sometimes we can't resist. This one is Pepper."

Kyle nodded at the puppy. "Very cute."

"Would you like to hold him?" Before Kyle could even process her question, Maureen dropped the furball into his arms. "He seems very social. He's at least part Border Collie. Very smart breed."

As if confirming her description of him, the puppy put his front paws on Kyle's chest and reached up to lick his chin.

"He likes you." The teen took a step back. A subtle move to make the puppy more his than hers. The girl was good. And poor Kyle didn't seem to know what to do next.

The slow smile that took over his face confirmed what Addison had already begun to think—Kyle had a gentler side that she wouldn't mind getting to know a whole lot better. For now, the least she could do was step out to the lobby and save him before Maureen had him driving home with as many critters as would fit in that sleek sports car.

By the time she'd settled the kittens in a crate and made her way into the lobby, Kyle was juggling the squirming pup on his casted arm, scratching behind the puppy's ears with his good hand, and laughing from deep in his gut. Somehow he was even more handsome than he'd been the last time she'd seen him. "Hello."

His head snapped around, and shifting the puppy to hold him more securely, Kyle smothered his laughter and cleared his throat. "Hello to you."

Maureen glanced from one to the other, frowned momentarily, then shrugging, took another step back. "I've got work to do. You got this?"

"Yeah. I got this." Addison nodded.

They waited till Maureen had left the lobby.

"Looks like you've got a new friend." She stepped forward and scratched the puppy's head.

"He's cute. But not appropriate for a man who travels a lot, and when home, lives on a boat." Slowly, Kyle set the puppy back in the pen with the other dogs.

"A boat around here?"

He shook his head. "No. I'm visiting my grandparents."

Kyle was probably the first person she'd ever met who actually lived on a houseboat. She wasn't so sure what to make of it, but for a man who didn't have room in his life— or on his boat—for a dog, he kept his gaze on the pup for a few long moments like a mother reassuring herself on the first day of kindergarten that her child would be just fine.

"So, what brings you here? Would a kitten be more practical?"

"Surrounded by water? I doubt it." He chuckled and shook his head, then ran his hand across the back of his neck and let his elbow hang. "I, uh, was thinking about the other day and all that I put you through."

She nodded, not knowing where he was going with this.

"I decided that a lone lunch wasn't enough of an apology."

"It wasn't?" She thought his paying for all the repairs was not only appropriate, but gracious. Still, she wondered what else he had in mind.

"If you have some time when you're done here, I'd love another chance to thank you. Maybe over a real dinner?"

As if the lunch they shared was fake. "I might have some time."

His smile brightened and not till this very second when his hand fell to his side did she realize how nervous he'd been about asking her out. Wasn't that just one more sweet thing to add to the list of who Kyle was really.

"Good." He smiled. "What time do you get off today?"

"Oh. Today?"

"Is tomorrow better?" His smile slipped just a smidge.

"No." She'd just churn herself into a nervous wreck waiting for the hours to pass. "I'm a volunteer. I can leave any time I want. I just have a few things I'd like to finish cleaning up. How about you give me another hour and then I can meet you somewhere?"

He shook his head. "My grandfather would hand me my head on a silver platter. How about I pick you up here in an hour?"

"Better yet," she spun around and pulled a note pad from the reception desk and scribbled down her mom's address, "pick me up here in an hour and half." She most certainly did not want to go to a 'real' dinner smelling like she'd been scrubbing up a dog shelter.

"I can do that." He nodded at her, then glancing over at the puppies, he smiled and took a backward step. "An hour and a half. Dress casual."

"Got it. Casual."

"See you in an hour."

"And a half," she added.

"Right." He backed all the way out the door and reaching his car, waved at her and slid into the driver seat.

A blue Mercedes, a red sports car, just how many cars did this guy have?

CHAPTER FIVE

One of the things that Kyle Baron was most well known for was his ability to enjoy life. Not just because he played for a living, not that everybody would agree racing cars is the same thing as playing, but because of his ability to appreciate the simpler pleasures of daily life.

His impromptu date with Addison was a prime example. He really wanted to take her somewhere with great food and an atmosphere conducive to getting to know her better. Some people would try to impress her with flash, but he found the perfect low key steakhouse to do the trick.

Taking note of the address on his GPS, he turned into the narrow driveway of the small craftsman home. In an older established neighborhood, the house was tidy and well kept. Somehow that did not surprise him. Pretty pink, purple, orange, and red mounds of flowers lined the beds in front of the home. His grandmother would know exactly what they were. He wondered who in the family had the green thumb.

"Hello." Addison closed the front door behind her and stopped at the edge of the wrap around front porch. "You're punctual."

"No value in being late."

Addison chuckled as she came down the steps. "No. I suppose there isn't."

"Are you hungry?"

"Actually, I'm famished."

"Good." He opened the passenger door for her and once she was snugly inside, circled around to the driver side.

Strapped into her seatbelt, Addison seemed to study the

interior of the car. "I know this is none of my business, but just how many cars do you own?"

The question made him chuckle. "Actually, I own three, but none of these are mine."

"Excuse me?"

"I guess I should explain." He pulled away from the curb.

Smiling sweetly, she nodded. "Please do."

"The blue Mercedes is my sister Eve's car. Because of my wrist, I can't drive a manual for now. So, my sister and I traded cars. To go to the shelter, I borrowed my brother Craig's car. And this baby," he tapped his hand on the dashboard of the plush luxury sedan, neglecting to mention he'd burned rubber racing to the ranch and back in time, "belongs to my grandfather. I thought you would appreciate something with more comfort."

"That was very thoughtful of you. Thanks."

"So you approve of my choice?"

"Tradition and luxury go hand in hand with Cadillac."

"My grandfather is allergic to foreign cars."

"Literally or figuratively?"

Kyle chuckled. "Figuratively. He spent a lot of years in the military and is very pro Made in the USA."

"Even without a military background, a lot of people are pro Made in the USA."

"Agreed." His grandparents had several pet projects, buying American-made was top of the list.

Earlier, in an effort not to drive halfway across the state of Texas, he'd researched the most popular steakhouse within a reasonable distance from Addison's mom's house and one of his favorite restaurants in Houston had an establishment not too far away. "You mentioned you were a carnivore, so I'm hoping a steakhouse is okay."

"More than okay." A slow soft smile appeared. "It was sweet of you to remember."

An embarrassed blush touched his cheeks before he shot her a sideways glance. "Ribeye or New York Strip?"

"Ribeye. More flavor."

His head bobbed. "Rare or well done?"

"Medium. I like the flavor but would prefer it if my dinner didn't moo."

Again, she made him laugh. "Fair enough."

"And you?" she asked.

"Medium rare."

"I suppose that's better than tartare." She tugged on the seatbelt to loosen its hold on her, and shifted around to face him. "So, just how many siblings do you have?"

"Six. My mom and dad had five kids. My brother Chase is the oldest. He recently married. Then my brother Mitch, he's a widower."

"Oh, I'm sorry."

Kyle nodded. They all were. Abbie was a great gal and perfect for Mitch. She could wear all the family hats, politician's wife, rancher's wife, Fortune 500 wife, and the best part, the wife of the ordinary man who to this day still adored her. "I'm next in line, then my brother Craig."

"That would be the red sports car."

"It would. The youngest of my mom's brood is Eve."

She bobbed her head. "Blue Mercedes."

"Correct."

"You said six siblings."

"My parents divorced and Dad remarried and had my sister Paige. Then when that marriage fell apart he married again and had my sister Siobhan."

"And that marriage stuck?"

The car rolled to a stop at the red light near the main drag in town, and he turned to her. "Afraid not. Much to my grandparents' chagrin, Dad is on wife number four."

"How's that working out for him?"

"Jury's still out. So far so good." He chuckled inwardly. He was definitely giving his father the benefit of the doubt. The man was clueless when it came to being a good husband and father. Kyle would have thought with the Governor as an example that his father would have been a little better at playing both parts.

"Maybe for your father the fourth time is the charm."

"Would be nice." He really did want to see his father happy, but he'd given up on the man truly settling down two wives ago. Though it did seem that he and a few of his siblings might not have been standing in line when God handed out the settle down and raise your own family genes. "What about you? Do you have siblings?"

"Only child."

The light turned green and he took off a little faster than he'd meant to. Luxury sedans weren't designed for drag racing, but that didn't mean that this particular sedan didn't have a little kick to it. The perk of a small Texas town is that getting from point A to point B doesn't take nearly as long as it does in big cities like Dallas or Houston. Turning the corner, he pulled into the parking lot of the famed Texas steakhouse.

"Oh, I've always wanted to try this place out."

That was good news for him. Even though the lot had plenty of spaces, he pulled up to the valet, handed over his keys, hurried around to meet Addison by her car door, and led her inside.

"Welcome to the Bluebonnet. Two for dinner?" A young girl, probably from the local college, hugged two menus to her chest.

"Yes. Please."

The kid nodded and gestured for them to follow her. To Kyle's delight they were led to a quiet booth near the back of the restaurant. He liked being able to see everything that was going on in the establishment and he loved the privacy the booth allowed them.

"You looked good with that puppy." Addison smiled coyly over the edge of her menu.

"The puppy was cute. He'd probably make anyone look good."

"Maybe." She returned her attention to the menu. "Do you have animals?"

He shook his head. "I travel too much. It wouldn't be fair to a pet to be left alone for long days or kenneled for long trips. My job takes me all over the world from week to week."

That caught her attention. Her gaze shot up fast and leveled with his. "I used to think it would be fun to have a job that travels the world, but I have a few friends with jobs that require travel, and tourism is never part of the agenda."

He shrugged. "Work is work no matter where you are in the world. But some places, it's impossible not to enjoy the pace of the local flavor."

So," she set the menu to one side of the table, "what exactly do you do?"

There was no reason not to tell her what he did for a living, but he didn't want to share that information just yet. People so often had a tendency to judge a book by its cover. Or in his case, the man by his job. He really wanted her to have a chance to like him for who he was, not for what he did, and especially not for what family he belonged to. He'd had his share of race car groupies or girls with dollar signs in their eyes. If she didn't recognize him yet, he wanted to keep it that way at least a little longer.

"Are you ready to order?" A waitress, who didn't look any older than the hostess who had seated them, stood by their table.

Saved by the proverbial bell. If he was lucky maybe Addison would forget her question at least until dessert.

"That was the best dinner I've had in forever." More than once Addison had wanted to take her mom to dinner at the Bluebonnet but it was one of the most expensive places in town and some unexpected expense always popped up and drained her budget. When Kyle originally ran her off the road in a Mercedes, she'd guessed that it was unlikely he was on a tight budget. By the time he'd picked her up in a third car, she had no clue what she was dealing with, but now she was sure if nothing else, this guy wasn't counting his pennies. Something she was going to be doing more carefully until she got a new job.

"Very glad you enjoyed it."

"I really did. That burnt corn was amazing, and wasn't burnt at all! So glad you talked me into it despite the name."

She'd been tempted to play with her food a little longer. The evening had gone by too quickly. The conversation had shifted from one thing to another seamlessly. She'd laughed, smiled, and truly enjoyed the company. Waiting for the car, she wished she weren't stuffed so she could have ordered more food to drag the night out a little longer.

Kyle closed the car door behind her and handing the valet a tip, climbed into the driver's seat. Both of them strapped in, he twisted in his seat. "You up for staying out a little longer?"

"I've got no place to be in the morning." For the first time since losing her job, she was actually pleased she didn't have to deal with the alarm clock.

"Great." He pulled onto the main drag and turned left. "A buddy of mine has been expanding his business outside of Houston the last few years. He just opened a place not too far from your mother's."

"What kind of place?"

He eyed her carefully. So much so, she had to make a conscious effort not to squirm under the scrutiny. "I think I'll leave it a surprise."

"Well, you did good picking a place for dinner." She leaned back comfortably in the seat. "Guess I can trust you for after dinner entertainment."

"Thank you." He grinned at her and she couldn't resist grinning back. She felt like a teen going to her first dance. Maybe better.

Another few minutes and they'd barely crossed over the city limit when Kyle pulled into the parking lot. She stared up at the sign and let out a good laugh. "Putt putt golf?"

"Absolutely." He climbed out of the car and hurried around the hood. "It's lots of fun."

Sure it was. When she was ten. But no one had ever said she wasn't a team player.

"Can you play with that cast?" She picked out a putter and watched Kyle weigh and swing every club one handed before choosing. She'd assumed they were all alike. Even if she took the time to swing and test it, she wouldn't have a clue what she'd be looking for.

"I guess we'll find out."

"Do you play putt putt often?"

He shrugged. "My job keeps me traveling most of the time."

"You mentioned that before." A true gentleman, Kyle let her go first. She stood at the foot of the first hole, looked down at the ball and wondering if she'd picked the right putter or not, swung lightly sending the ball almost all the way to the hole. A second careful stroke and the golf ball fell into the desired spot. Surprisingly pleased with herself, she spun around grinning and waved Kyle on. "Your turn."

"Very good." He nodded at her as he switched places, eyeing his destination carefully. Too carefully. He half swung a few times. Seemed to almost sway left then right, looked up and down a few times and finally tapped the ball just hard enough to make it up the narrow runway and drop clean into the hole.

"Wow. And one handed too."

He shrugged. "Beginner's luck."

Somehow she didn't believe that for a minute. Maybe the one handed part, but round after round, she managed to sink the ball in only two or three strokes, and Kyle had occasionally needed a second stroke, but never a third. Holding her club tightly in front of her, she stood to the side and watched Kyle analyze, consider, shimmy from left to right before swinging up and back and once again sinking the ball in a single stroke. He smiled and waved her over to the next area. A smooth section of putting green with a pond and turtle shells between them and the next hole.

Less than halfway to the end of the course, Addison took her time. Studied the course more carefully, though she wasn't totally sure what exactly she was studying. She considered the weight of her club, not heavy, and the distance the ball needed to travel, and realized as an engineer, she should be able to figure this out. She did a little makeshift swinging and then with an earnest effort, wielded the club, sending the ball across the green, over the pond, and swooshing into the hole. "I did it!" Throwing both arms up in the air, she spun around to face Kyle.

"Finally, a hole in one."

"Well done." He gave her an enthusiastic high five and a grin to match.

The next round she'd done it again, and then once again after that. Each time Kyle cheered her on, but she could see the intensity in his efforts increasing with every new stroke. When what should have been an easy shot for him, skirted around the hole without actually falling in, she could hear him grumbling under his breath as he marched heavily over to knock the ball into the hole. It seemed Mr. Kyle had a bit of a competitive streak and she was having even more fun inching her score closer to his. "Care to make a little wager as to who's going to win this match?"

One eyebrow lifted high on his forehead. "I didn't peg you for a gambler."

She shrugged. "I'm not really. But according to my assessments, if I don't cave under pressure, I stand an excellent chance of beating you."

"Excellent, huh?" His grin gave an extra sparkle to his eyes.

"That's how I see it." She crossed her arms and gave him a minute to pretend to think about it. He was right about one thing for sure. She most definitely was not a gambler. Risks and bets and chances were not her strong suit, but watching him treat this course like he were vying for the green jacket made her chuckle to herself. There were many sides to this man and she was most definitely hoping she'd get more opportunity to enjoy all of them.

CHAPTER SIX

"You're up early." Eve looked up from the comfy chair by the fireplace. "You came home early last night too. I thought you had a hot date."

"After midnight I turn into a pumpkin."

Kyle's sister set her book on her lap and gave him a hearty laugh from deep in her belly. He absolutely loved it when his sister laughed. Not a sweet smiling, be cordial and polite chuckle that was required when somebody said something they thought was funny. The sunny side of her disposition could brighten anyone's day, but her laugh, an earnest laugh, always lifted his soul.

Eve shoved to her feet and sidled up by her brother, studying his face. "Whoever she is, I like her."

"Excuse me?"

"You look peaceful. I don't see that often in your eyes. Actually," she smiled softly, "I don't think I ever see peace in your eyes."

"Did it occur to you that maybe it's peaceful to be home surrounded by family?"

"Hmm." His sister pressed her lips together tightly, lifted her gaze to the ceiling and then with a casual shrug, shook her head and leveled her gaze with his and smiled. "Nope."

"Comedienne." He grabbed a cup of coffee and took a seat across from Eve.

"Not eating?"

"I will." He blew into the dark liquid. "I've got a breakfast meeting with some PR folks and then I have... plans."

"Plans?" Eve raised her brows at him and grinned.

"Sounds…interesting. Wouldn't happen to have anything to do with last night's date?"

"And if it did?"

Eve burst out laughing. "Do I get to tell the Governor?"

"You do not." Kyle forgot to blow on the coffee and swallowed the too hot brew quickly. "I don't need you making a mountain out of a mole hill."

"Got it. No mountain building."

Walking into the room with a frown on his face, Mitch reached for a mug and the coffee pot. "Are we building a mountain, or a hotel on the mountain?"

"Neither." Kyle pushed away from the table. "Our beloved sister is in a mood, and I have an appointment. Will see you all for dinner."

Lifting her cup to her lips, Eve eyed her brother over the rim. "Maybe."

Normally, Kyle loved when his sister teased her brothers. For a super smart chemist, she had a great way of being down to earth and down right fun. But he hoped she wasn't still in a teasing mood when he got home tonight. He wasn't up for the third degree, and didn't want to make more of his—what…relationship? Did a dinner date and putt putt golf count as a relationship? Whatever it was, he'd rather not share this budding *possible* relationship—at least for now. Maybe a hint here or there to his grandfather, but for now, he wanted to keep Addison to himself.

For someone who was unemployed and unsure of her future, Addison felt as though she walked on air. She knew so little about Kyle, yet was completely smitten. All she knew for sure was that she had way more fun playing golf last night with him than she'd had when she was ten.

"You look pleased with yourself." Her mother carried a hot cup of coffee in her hand. "I gather you had a nice time last night?"

"I did. I really did."

"Well, don't sound so surprised." Her mom chuckled. "People are allowed to have fun every once in a while."

"Are you implying that I don't have fun?"

"In a word? Yes. You graduated at the top of your class, and I'm so proud of you for all that you've accomplished in a man's world. But darling, you're just a tad too serious for someone as young as you are. You've never taken a real vacation that didn't involve reorganizing your closet or scrubbing grout. Maybe you should take advantage of this extra time on your hands and find a couple of girlfriends and go to Mexico."

"They have cartels in Mexico."

"And sunshine and music and tequila," her mom almost whined.

"And crime, and kidnappings, and don't forget Montezuma's revenge."

Her mom sighed and cupped her hand on her daughter's chin. "Honey, I love you, but loosen up a little. Trust me. Life is better when you laugh." Giving her a light kiss on the cheek, her mother turned on her heel and headed to her in home office to start her work day.

Maybe her mother was right. Not about Mexico, but about laughing more. She really had enjoyed herself last night, especially when she'd come from behind and beat Kyle. He was a good sport about it, but she could see toward the end of the game that the man did not like losing. She had a feeling there was a lot of complexity under the carefree surface that Kyle displayed. And she was most definitely looking forward to learning more of those complexities when he picked her up this afternoon. She had no idea what he had planned or where they were going, but she had a strong feeling that it would be more of that fun her mom talked about.

His day was not going according to plan. Kyle had woken later than usual, done a little verbal sparring with his sister over hot coffee, and then spent the remainder of the morning listening to his manager carry on as if he'd broken his neck not his wrist.

"Whatever you do, do not take anymore chances. The team is good, but they're not you."

"Yes, Gilbert."

"I don't like the sound of that."

"I'm agreeing with you. What's not to like?"

One eyebrow raised, his business manager since almost his first race shook his head. "I might as well be talking to a wall."

Kyle said nothing as the man standing next to him in the parking lot slid into the driver side of his practical sedan.

"Just try not to get yourself killed. Please."

"I promise." Kyle remained standing in the lot as the sedan pulled away. Now he was off to pick up his date. He had no idea how Addison was going to react, if she would enjoy herself as much as she had last night. At least he thought her smiles and laughter were sincere. But putt putt was a slow, easy game. He didn't have a clue how she'd react to a little speed.

The plan was to pick her up at her mother's. Truth was, he was putting plenty of miles on his car. At least his friend's place of business was on the north side of town, less driving. Glancing at his broken wrist out of habit, he blew out a heavy sigh and turned the other arm instead to look at the time. This dumb wrist couldn't heal fast enough. If he stepped on the gas, he'd probably get there on time.

Once again, after breaking the speed barriers he'd just promised Gilbert he wouldn't do, he pulled into the driveway and took a deep breath. For some ridiculous reason, he was a little nervous. Not sure why. Jitters was not territory he was used to. Slamming the car door shut behind him, he took the porch steps two at a time. His hand raised to rap on the door, it swung open and Addison stood smiling at him.

"Sorry I'm a little late."

"Not at all." She turned to pull the door closed. "Where

are we going today?"

"It's a surprise." He truly hoped that he wasn't out of his mind and about to scare her away. "We're heading back toward Houston. A buddy of mine has a little place that I think you might enjoy."

"You are full of mystery, aren't you?"

"Am I?" He waited for her to slide into the passenger side of his grandfather's sedan and hurried around to his side of the car. "Sorry. That wasn't my intent."

"Okay. Then where are we going?"

"North Side Tracks."

Her nose crinkled. "Tracks? As in railroad?"

"Not that kind of track."

"Then what?"

He turned to see her face. "Go-karts."

"Excuse me?" Now her brows rose high on her forehead, making her eyes round as saucers.

There was no stopping the chuckle that erupted at the look on her face. "Surprise."

"Are you kidding?" Her expression shifted from shock to curiosity.

"Nope." He turned onto the highway and resisted the urge to press the pedal to the ground at the clear road ahead. "You seemed to enjoy last night. I thought this might be something fun."

"I did have fun last night, but go-karts?"

He pushed the car a little faster. "You'll love it. Trust me."

"Uh oh." She chuckled. "'Trust me,' polite vernacular for something else?"

Laughing with her, he shook his head. "I'm serious. It will be fun."

"Somehow I doubt whiplash would be fun."

"Whiplash?"

"Yeah, from all those crazy kids banging into you and everyone else."

"That's bumper cars, not go-karts."

"Oh."

"Wait and see. If you don't love it, we can do

something easier, like the arcade."

"You really like to play, don't you?"

He nodded. "My whole life I promised myself I would always have fun."

"I can see that." She shifted in her seat again and he did his best to keep the conversation light. Hopefully he hadn't misjudged, but he was convinced underneath that austere engineer façade was a lady who really wanted to have a little fun.

CHAPTER SEVEN

In front of the building, he pulled into the first space in a nearly empty parking lot.

The entire rest of the drive Addison wondered what had she gotten herself into. She should be home sending out resumes, talking with headhunters, anything besides playing at a go-kart track. "Not a lot of people today?"

Hurrying around to open her door, Kyle stood back. "That's because they're not open for another hour or so."

"Oh. We're early." It made no sense that he was rushing to get here so they could wait around for another hour.

He shook his head. "My buddy is expecting us."

At the front door, Kyle tapped on the glass and a tall, middle aged gentleman came to the door. "Good to see you, man."

Kyle and his friend gave each other a manly hug that consisted mostly of slaps on the back.

"Addison, this is Lee."

"Nice to meet you." She stretched out her hand.

"Likewise."

Stepping aside, Kyle gestured for her to go in before him, but spoke to Lee. "Thanks for opening early."

"We can't have you racing against the kiddos. I don't have enough security around here."

Kyle smiled coyly, but neither agreed nor disagreed. To her the comment made no sense. Not racing the kids did, but needing security most definitely did not.

Lee led the way through the raceway. "The bullpen is this way."

Not sure what she was in for, the word bullpen did little to paint a better picture of what was ahead of them. As they crossed an arcade section, neither of the men paid any attention to various games filling the large area. At the rear of the building a few teens were busying themselves straightening up, probably getting ready for the day's business. Out the back doors, his buddy walked them down a chute that reminded her of something a bull at the rodeo might make his way through. At the end the man stopped in front of a row of low to the ground go-karts. She'd never seen one up close before, but this had to be what Kyle had brought her here for.

"They're a nice color. Striking shade of blue." It was a dumb thing to say, but the only thing she could think of.

Lee laughed. "My wife picked it out."

"Why are some of the karts red?"

"Speed," Lee explained. "We get a lot of young teens in here so the majority of our cars don't travel at more than 25 or 30 miles per hour. Those are the red karts."

She nodded. Though nothing about a bunch of pre-teens flying around a track at 30 miles an hour seemed like a good idea to her.

"The blue ones are specialty karts that can go a more entertaining sixty miles per hour."

She gave a slow nod. Staring down at the pretty blue karts, other than liking the color, she was still baffled as to why anyone would want to drive that fast in these race car wannabes. She could picture the thing whirling around the bend, and without doors or a roof, the driver flying one way as the car sped on in the opposite direction.

"They're all ready for you." Lee waved an arm in the direction of the blue karts.

"For me?" She looked to Kyle then Lee. "Shouldn't I be using one of the red karts? You know, like the other kids?"

Lee looked to Kyle then back to her. "You can go as fast or slow as you want. I just happen to know that our friend here is going to want to go faster than the red karts."

"He's right. You don't have to go any faster than you want but it's going to be fun. You'll see."

He used that word fun an awful lot. "I don't know."

"It's perfectly safe," Lee reassured.

"These suckers are awfully low to the ground." She stared at what looked like a dune buggy that someone let all the air out of the tires.

"Easier to get in and out of. Especially for the younger kids."

Kyle came up beside her. "Make yourself comfortable. The safety harness will protect you better than a car seat cradles a baby. You'll notice the pedal on the left is red. That's the brake. The green one on the right is—"

"The gas pedal."

He nodded. "If for any reason the car stops running or you spin out—"

"Spin out?" Her voice squeaked out an octave or two higher than usual.

"It's unlikely," he continued. "If it does just don't get out. Someone will run out to get you going again."

Everything he said came out so matter of fact that it should have been reassuring, but it wasn't, and the amused smile teasing his friend's lips wasn't helping calm her nerves any. Couldn't they just go back to putt putt?

"Come on. Sit." Kyle held his hand out to her.

Slowly, she inched forward, then sucking in a fortifying breath, settled into the single seat. She knew it was low to the ground, but she felt like she was sitting on the floor.

"Not so bad, huh?" Lee grinned at her so brightly anyone would think he'd gifted her an expensive sports car.

All she could do was force a smile and nod.

Kyle leaned across her to strap her in. Single handed, he tugged at the shoulder straps, checked the tension, then nodded and stepped back. "We'll pull out, do our laps, and when you've had enough, you pull into the pit."

Pit. She held back a sigh. Did she want to embarrass herself and ask what the pit was? Unless she wanted to drive round and round for the rest of the day, she'd better get over the need to look like she knew what was happening and speak up.

"The pits have three lanes." For a split second she wondered if Kyle could read her mind. "Each one has a divider curb. That will keep everyone safe, even though there are only the two of us out here now."

"Depending on how long you two circle round," Lee interrupted, "more folks may be on the track."

Kyle nodded and tapped the metal bar up and over her head. "Give me a minute to get into my kart."

"Shouldn't I be wearing a helmet or something?"

"Despite what my friend here would like to think," Lee skewered Kyle with a teasing glare, "this isn't a Formula One track. You'll be fine."

Easy for him to say. Hands on the steering wheel, her palms were sweating. This was crazy. She enjoyed relaxing pastimes that challenged her mind—something she could control. If only his idea of fun had been Trivia Time at a local pub, or maybe a Scrabble tournament at the library. Gripping the handle more tightly, her fingers almost cramping from the pressure, she swallowed hard. This is supposed to be fun. For heaven's sake, kids did this all the time. She could do this. Waiting a minute for Kyle in front of her to lead the way onto the track, when his car moved, she slowly stepped on the gas, almost surprised when the toy-like car actually moved.

As soon as Kyle's kart hit the track, he took off, bad wrist and all. From what she'd seen so far, it was going to take more than a cast to slow this man down. She had no idea if it was because she was so low to the ground, or so unprotected from the elements, but barely stepping on the green pedal she felt like she was flying. Her heart raced faster than the toy car. It didn't take very long for her to creep partway around and then have Kyle come up on her side, wave a thumbs up and a smile at her, before hitting the gas and rushing past her.

For a long moment she stared after his rear bumper. A feeling of being left behind simply because she was a girl roiled in her gut. She'd raced to the top of her engineering classes from sheer will and effort. Would it really kill her to chase after Kyle? With a new determination, she pressed harder on the pedal and the kart took off with a shot. Kyle was only slightly ahead of her, so she pushed harder on the pedal. On his tail, she found herself pushing down more on the pedal in an effort to overtake him. They'd done two more laps when he must have eased back because suddenly, wind flying in her hair she was breezing past him. For another two laps, pressing the pedal to the floor, leaning into the turn with every curve, she spotted Lee waving her over to what she suspected was the pit.

Easing back on the pedal, she slowed slightly, braking as she got closer and glided in. Careful not to bump and ride over the curbs. She could hear Kyle pulling into the pit behind her. Fumbling to undo the safety harness, she finally unfastened the latch and practically sprang out of the car. Spinning about and spotting Kyle already outside of his kart and grinning at her, she darted down the narrow concrete curb and throwing her hands up in the air, squealed, "I won!"

For so much of his earlier instructions, Addison's narrowed gaze and clenched teeth had him second guessing this whole idea of go-karts. In the back of his mind, with every word he'd uttered on how to safely ride the track, he'd battered back and forth if perhaps something a little slower paced would have been more appropriate. Since Lee had everything ready for them, and she was willing to at least try, he didn't change his mind right away and hoped bringing her here hadn't been the friendship equivalent of shooting himself in the foot.

But just now, the look on her face when she got out of the go-kart was worth every second he'd been fraught with concern. Watching her bounce up and down with excitement like a little kid gave him as big a rush as crossing the finish line at two hundred miles per hour. Now all he could think about was what to do next to make her smile like that again.

"Can we do that again?" Addison spun around and faced Lee. "That was so much fun."

Lee dipped his chin in a curt nod. "Yes, ma'am. That's

what keeps us in business."

Part of Kyle certainly understood the adrenaline rush that came with the need for speed, but another part of him hadn't anticipated her wanting to race again. "You really want to take another run?"

Her head bobbed up and down rapidly. "Absolutely."

Lee turned his wrist, stared briefly at his watch, then looked back up at her. "We open in a few minutes. Are you up to more than two cars on the track?"

Sudden blank expression replaced the exuberance of only a moment ago. She did that cute little thing nibbling on the corner of her lower lip before slowly nodding. "I'd like to try."

Kyle resisted the urge to shout out *atta girl*, and looked to his friend. "Do we need to switch to the slower karts?"

"No. I've already sold tickets for the faster karts. This track will be designated for the blue karts."

"All right then." He slapped his hands together and rubbed vigorously. "Then let's go."

Another run around the track, this time with a handful more cars in the lanes, and he was truly impressed with how Addison took the turns and kept in her lane. One car spun out and everything slowed as a few of the teens they'd seen earlier ran out and putting their backs into it, turned the car in the right direction and shoved it on its way.

He missed being behind the wheel of a real car. One that could fly like the wind while hugging the asphalt like a long-lost lover. This little roundabout served to wet his whistle and rue the soap bar that took out his wrist. When he spotted Addison following the other karts into the pit, he slowed and rolled in behind her. Letting one of the teens help her out of the kart, she shook her hair out and finger-combed the damage wind and speed had done, and reeled around to face him as he climbed out.

"I can't believe I have never done this before."

"You're a natural." He looked around for any signs of his friend.

Arms linked, they crossed the large arcade area and Addison's steps slowed, bringing them to a stop.

Trying to follow the direction of her gaze, he couldn't quite figure out what had caught her eyes and brought her to a halt. "What is it?"

Her head slightly tipped, she shook it and smiled. "I guess there are all kinds."

It finally struck him what she had noticed. A young girl in a massive purple ball gown with layers of netted fabric, enough sparkles to light the sky, and an honest to heavens tiara on her head sat behind the wheel of one of the games. "A Quinceañera."

She nodded. "I couldn't have been more surprised to have a bride and groom in full regalia. I wonder if this is the after party, or a detour on the way to the party?"

Kyle shrugged. "Not a clue. I suppose it does take all kinds."

"Yep." She smiled up at him. "Now what?"

"I don't know about you but I'm starved."

"Racing does work up an appetite, doesn't it?"

"This is nothing. When a racer is driving at two hundred miles an hour, the g-forces do a number on your body. A driver can lose up to five pounds just from sweating."

"Oh, I know a few women who would pay big bucks to lose five pounds in an afternoon."

Kyle couldn't help but laugh out loud. That wouldn't be the first time he'd heard a woman say that and yet, it still struck him as the funniest darn thing he'd heard in a long while.

Spotting Lee near the front of the establishment, Kyle thanked him, slapped his buddy on the back and escorted Addison to the car. Opting for a quick drive-thru burger, by the time they reached her home, they were well fed, and despite a little conversational footwork to deflect questions of his career, they were well informed of basics like favorite color, favorite song, favorite movie, and shared more than a few laughable moments in memory of their most awkward years.

"So," Kyle parked in the driveway and undid his safety belt, "do you have plans for Saturday?"

Wary eyes narrowed as she softly asked, "What did you

have in mind?"

Another smile tugged at the corner of his lips. He seemed to be smiling a lot more often of late. "Would you believe another surprise?"

"I don't think I can take another surprise." She chuckled, shook her head, and unlatched her belt.

"Fair enough." He shrugged. "What do you think of sailing?"

"Never been."

He'd hoped for a simple yes or no. "Would you like to sail with me?"

It took her a few beats too many to respond. He was almost all set to backpedal and suggest something more simple like a movie or maybe bowling when that easy smile reappeared and she nodded her head. "I have a feeling it's going to be a lot of fun."

He grinned. "You're going to love it." Now all he had to do was be patient till Saturday came along. Slamming his door shut behind him, he circled round to meet her by her door. Suddenly Saturday seemed too far away. And wasn't that something new? Growing more consumed by a woman instead of growing away. What other surprises did Addison Ray hold for him?

CHAPTER EIGHT

The last few days had been the slowest in Kyle's life. He couldn't remember the last time he looked forward to spending time with a woman outside the bedroom. Heck, he couldn't remember the last time he'd enjoyed just sitting and talking to a woman he wasn't related to, ever, especially not time after time. They'd been together for lunch, dinner, long drives, and now on the road to where the sailboat was docked, his interest wasn't ebbing in the slightest. If anything, Addison was working her way firmly under his skin.

"A penny for your thoughts?" Buckled in on the passenger side of the car, Addison's smile was bright enough to light up both seaboards.

"Not worth that much."

"Ouch." She chuckled. "That bad?"

This time he smiled at her. "Not bad at all. I was hoping that you're going to enjoy sailing even more than putt putt or go-karts."

"I hope you're right." Her hands on her lap, for the first time since he'd picked her up, he noticed she was wringing her fingers together.

"Have you ever been on a boat before?" He couldn't believe that it hadn't occurred to him to ask sooner.

Her head whipped left then right quickly. "Afraid not."

"There's nothing to be nervous about." Slowly, he reached over and momentarily squeezed her hand. "The sailboat is perfectly safe."

Her hands stilled and she bobbed her head. "I'm sure it is. What's the boat's name again?"

"*Fidelis*. That's Latin for faithful." Despite her efforts

at being casual, he could tell she was stifling a wave of nerves. "Would you prefer we did something else? Something on dry land? Maybe bowling?"

Her smile returned. "No, I'm a terrible bowler."

"Then I guess sailing it is."

Keeping her gaze straight ahead and her hands remaining still, she nodded, not looking completely convinced, but less nervous nonetheless. "Sailing it is."

For the remaining short distance to the marina, they rode along in what his sister's novels always referred to as a comfortable silence. Up until now he hadn't really given that phrase any real thought, but at the moment it made perfect sense. He didn't particularly care what she said, or when she said it, so long as she was with him.

Another few minutes and he turned the corner into the small parking lot. By the time he circled the car to open her door, she was already standing, one hand over her brows shading her eyes from the sun, staring off into the distance and all the boats docked. "Which one is the *Fidelis*?"

Because of its size, the *Fidelis* wasn't docked at this portion of the marina, but moored slightly offshore. He extended his arm away from where she was looking and pointed in the distance. "There she is."

He wished he'd had his phone out so he could have taken a photograph of her expression when she realized where he was pointing. Her jaw fell and her eyes popped open wide. "Oh, wow. That's bigger than I thought it was going to be."

Kyle didn't have the heart to tell her that when they got up close the *Fidelis* was going to look even bigger. "The family used to race her in the circuit regularly. She needs to be sleek enough for speed, but large enough to house the crew."

"How many crew?"

"Depends on the race. The longer the distance, the more people to rotate shifts."

She dipped her chin once. "Makes sense."

"Come this way." He extended his hand to her, together they walked to where the small dinghy waited for them.

Despite her minor case of nerves, she stepped into the dinghy with perfect ease. Anyone watching would have thought she'd done this often. As the small boat motored away from the dock and drew closer to the *Fidelis*, her eyes grew slightly larger. "She is beautiful."

He couldn't help but grin. "That she is. And she's yar. Every sailor's dream."

"Yar?" She turned to him.

"It's actually a rather old fashioned word, but since my grandfather is the one who taught us all how to sail, we still use it. Yar means quick and agile; easy to hand, reef and steer. There isn't a better word for it."

"And in a race that would be important." It wasn't a question.

Once on the boat, he waved at the captain and one of the deck hands. The captain and he had a short conversation about the plan for the afternoon and then he showed Addison around. Not that there was much to see on deck. The family had refitted the boat for comfort and leisure, but it was still a racing boat, which meant there wasn't really any place on deck to sit comfortably and enjoy the view.

"Well, this is different." She smiled and grabbed hold of the side for balance as she descended the opposing foot steps. Rather than having a full width step, each step was only half sized so as not to take up as much space below deck, but afford more stability than a rung ladder. "I don't know that I've ever seen stairs like this before."

"In a racing vessel everything has to be as compact and consolidated as you can get it. Streamlined in all aspects is the key to winning a race."

"Makes sense. It actually wouldn't be a half bad idea for confined spaces where architects and designers put those narrow spiral staircases."

Back on deck, he spoke again with the captain and then turned to Addison. "A few things I need to tell you before we shove off."

She nodded.

"First, this is a leisurely cruise but if we catch a good wind, this baby is designed for speed."

Again she dipped her chin.

"I don't want you to panic or get nervous if you feel the boat heeling."

"Heeling?"

Waving his arm from the elbow he demonstrated a forty-five degree angle. "Tilting."

"Tilting?" Her voice rose a notch.

"Yes. The sails will go almost horizontal. I don't think that will happen, but if it does, there's nothing to worry about."

"Oh-kay."

He chuckled at her hesitation. "Really. In a real race, for the cup, the sails often touch the water."

This time her eyes rounded showing a perfectly symmetrical ring of white around those deep blue circles he'd grown so fond of. "Now you're teasing me."

"Nope. But like I said, nothing to worry about."

Barely moving her mouth, she quietly muttered, "Nothing to worry about."

"I'm going to help the crew get her ready to sail." He walked her to the edge of the deck. "Go ahead and take a seat here, take your shoes off, and hang your legs over the side."

"Can't I just sit by where you are?"

He shook his head. "Not till you learn how to sail. For now, just make yourself comfortable here. As soon as we're done and the sails are hoisted up the mast, Tim will untie the mooring line and we can set sail." He watched her slowly ease herself down on the edge much the way an arthritic family pet would gingerly lower himself to the comfort of their soft bed. "Okay, now grab onto the lifeline."

One brow shot up in question.

"The rail. Until you get your sea legs, you're going to want to hold onto something and this is the best option."

She sucked in a deep breath and feet hanging over the side, curled her fingers around the thin wire rope that served as a railing and was probably praying she wasn't going to need a real lifeline.

From her tight hold, he could almost see the whites of her knuckles. He couldn't quite decide if he should chuckle at her efforts to keep a brave face or take her back to dry land. "Ready?"

Again, her chest heaved with another deep gulp of air and she nodded her head. "As ready as I'll ever be."

He certainly hoped so. "Then we're off!"

From what she understood, the two scraggly men moving about the deck were the regular crew of the sailboat, and at the moment, Kyle was their extra hand—literally, since whatever he seemed to do, he did with only his good arm. With her back to the crew, she had no idea exactly what they were doing, but she sucked in another long deep breath. At the same moment, a brisk gulf breeze washed over her, both refreshing and calming. She reminded herself that she had no reason to be nervous or concerned. So what if he had her sitting on the very edge with her legs dangling off the boat? He wasn't making her walk the plank, or setting her feet in cement.

The truth of the matter was that she was worrying unnecessarily and needed to get a grip. Both literally and figuratively. As she sat there talking herself off a terrified ledge, the boat began to move and once again she took a deep breath. Two more minutes and the boat was slowly making its way out to sea. Very slowly. So slowly that she relaxed her grip and shaking her head, silently chided herself once again for being so silly about it.

Another few minutes had passed and the boat seemed to be moving at a steady but reasonable pace. She dared to momentarily let go of the railing long enough to brush back a stray lock of hair. The boat seemed to pick up a little speed. Just enough for the water to make waves against them and tickle the bottoms of her feet, but not fast enough to bring her nerves front and center again.

"Feeling better?" His pant legs rolled midway up his

calves, he sat beside her, his legs dangling over the side.

"Was it that obvious?"

"To anyone with eyes." He chuckled. "I considered backing out."

Focusing on the horizon, she considered the breeze blowing, the swishing sound of water surrounding them, and the warm sun beating down on the sleek sailing vessel. "I'm glad you didn't. It's actually very nice."

Kyle bobbed his head. "There's something special about leaving the world behind and hanging out with Mother Nature."

"The only sad thing is that like it or not, at some point we have to return to reality."

"Is reality that bad?"

She shook her head. "Just a little tenuous."

"No luck with finding a job?"

"Not sure." She shifted, not feeling the need to hang on as tightly to the railing. "I've sent out enough resumes to fill a room."

"No responses?"

"Not yet. I know it can take a while. At least I got a nice severance package so I don't have to worry about paying bills or buying groceries." She stopped herself from adding *yet*. "From where I sit, you seem to have everything most people want. Money, family, friends. What are you escaping?"

"The noise."

That wasn't the answer she was expecting. Not that she was expecting anything in particular, but this was a bit of a surprise. "Care to clarify?"

The corners of his mouth lifting in a sweet smile, he chuckled. "Even though I'm as extroverted as they come, life in general is always moving. Phones are always ringing with a call, or dinging with a text, and we can't forget social media, or media in general. Then with a family as large as mine there's often some minor or major crisis and a call to arms for the family."

"That last part must be nice."

"The call to arms? You can thank having the clan run

by a former Marine for that."

"That, but having a family to rally at all. As an only child with only two first cousins who live in different states, well, when something goes awry, there's no cavalry coming to my aid."

"I can't even imagine. I may complain about my siblings, or cousins, with some regularity, but I can't fathom not having each and every one of them in my life." He shook his head. He was facing her, but his gaze was focused somewhere far off in the distance. She got the impression from the sad glimmer in his eyes that he wasn't looking forward but back. "Not very long ago I almost lost my youngest sister Siobhan. If not for my brother Chase's date, now his wife, we would have lost her way too young."

"How old is she now?"

He smiled. The twinkle returning to his eyes. "Twenty two, maybe twenty three. Hard to keep up. In my mind she's always sixteen and a bit of a firecracker. A car crashed into the hotel where my family was staying for a cousin's wedding and if not for CJ being a nurse, Siobhan would have bled out."

"Oh dear."

"That's one way to put it." Kyle slapped his good hand on his thigh and smiled brightly. "But no point in lingering on what might have been."

"Agreed."

"Mr. B?" One of the two men who had been at the wheel of the boat stood behind them. "Take a look port side."

Kyle looked over his shoulder and around the man behind them. As wide as his smile was, it expanded and that twinkle in his eyes exploded into a full on sparkle. "Too good to ignore."

"Thought you might think so." The guy sported the same sly grin that Kyle did.

She had no idea what they were talking about, but that serene calm feeling that had finally made itself at home deep inside her was suddenly washed aside by a flock of angry geese flapping about in the pit of her stomach.

CHAPTER NINE

"**N**ow that you have your sea legs." Kyle patted her knee and pushed to his feet.

"I have sea legs?" It was news to her.

"You do." He smiled. "That boat on our side has been egging us on for a little race."

"Race?" The word came out more like a squeak than verbal communication.

"Relax. A friendly race."

She wasn't so sure she wanted to know what an unfriendly race was.

"A few things you should know before we speed up."

Oh, there was another word she was not pleased to hear.

"It's a good day for a sail. When the winds kick in and we take off, there may be times, like I mentioned before, when it feels like we're going to tip over."

"Tip over!"

He held up his casted hand. "I said 'feels like'. We're not equipped to go fast enough for the sails to touch the water, so you need to reassure yourself no matter how far we lean, she's built for this. There will be no tipping over. I promise. But if the wind shifts we may have to tack—sorry, change the course of the boat by switching the position of the sails to the opposite side. So keep your eyes open and you may want to hold on tight again, because in a couple of minutes we're going to give that sucker a run for the money."

There was no need for him to tell her to hold on more tightly. The minute the word race had passed his lips, she'd grabbed the lifeline. When the words 'tip over' made an appearance, she'd gripped even more tightly. She had no idea what Kyle and the other two were doing but somehow the sail seemed…fuller, and before she could even think of asking to go below deck and maybe lie down, preferably away from windows, the boat was indeed picking up speed—quickly.

Wind whipped through her hair. The thought to have put it up in a clip crossed her mind, but she didn't dare let go of the rope. The water slapped high on the sides of the boat and splashed her feet more forcefully, leaving her torn between laughing and screeching. She found the nerve to look over her shoulder. Somehow Kyle managed to look stern and serious while laughing. How the three of them could walk on a boat bouncing over the waves was beyond her.

Another few minutes passed and the boat began leaning. Hard. She reminded herself of what he'd said, and mentally repeated, *this is okay, this is okay.* One more glance in their direction and the three men were firmly on their feet as if standing on flat dry land. Kyle stood behind the wheel while the other two moved about doing who knew what. She refrained from asking the obvious, shouldn't you have two good hands to control the steering wheel? Shifting his focus from the horizon, he looked toward the other boat that was sailing in the distance at the same rapid clip. Was the whole world nuts?

"You doing okay?" Kyle's voice carried against the sound of the wind whirling around her.

She wanted to yell back, but fearful it might come out as a blood curdling scream, all she could manage was a quick nod. The wind blew a wall of hair in her face and sucking in a deep breath, she dared to let go with one hand and tuck the strands behind her ear. Another minute or two and once again she couldn't see through the locks covering her eyes—not that not seeing clearly was necessarily a bad thing at the moment—but she tried blowing her hair away from her eyes. Convinced it was a losing battle and swiped it away again.

What was the definition of insanity? Doing the same thing over and over and expecting different results.

Frustrated by her hair blowing all around her face, she let go of the railing and hunted in her pockets for something to tie back the loose strands. No luck in her pockets, she shifted just enough to pull her purse close and rummaged for a clip. Triumphant, she grinned and scooped her hair away from her face and high on her head she snapped the clip in place creating a pony tail that probably made her look like Pebbles Flintstone, only right now she didn't care how she looked. As long as her hair was no longer whipping about her face, she was content.

Twisting around, she faced forward and reached for the railing when it struck her she was not hanging on. Not only was she not gripping the railing to save her life, she'd been moving about in an effort to keep her hair out of her eyes. The sailboat was still leaning to one side and for the first time in the last few minutes, she realized, they were flying. No longer afraid, she froze in place and turned to search out Kyle. Still at the wheel, he was focused on some distant point ahead. Curious now, she glanced over to the boat that had apparently started the whole racing thing. A colorful red and yellow sail, the boat was close on Kyle's heels and she realized, they were ahead.

A surge of excitement zipped through her. They were ahead. She flung around, and phone in hand, began snapping photos. Unlike a short while ago, the wind in her face was no longer intimidating but invigorating. Another look over her shoulder and the red and yellow sail was losing ground. They were winning! She couldn't believe she was thinking this, but facing Kyle she actually shouted, "Faster!"

Ignoring a challenge to a good race had never been something Kyle was very good at. If it involved speed and a chance to show what the Baron stable of sailboats and cars could do, he was all in. Ever since the *Fidelis* had been retired from racing and docked in Texas, the Kincaid boys were always Jonesing for a race. It didn't hurt that their father had enough money to indulge them in more than just fast cars, boats, and women. Though Kyle was pretty sure most of the interest had as much to do with Kyle and his career as it did wanting to outrun a former America's Cup champion vessel.

Skipping over the waves, close enough to the water to reach over and touch if he wanted, always made for a good day. He probably shouldn't have taken on the Kincaids with Addison on board. From the second she stepped onto the boat he knew she wasn't comfortable. The way she hung onto the rails told him more than words, so when he heard her screaming faster, his skipper could have blown in his direction and knocked him overboard.

Not only was she cheering them on, she'd let go of the rail and scooted over so she was balancing herself while taking pictures. He thought little could shock him, but she had done just that. With a short gesture, he had the skipper take over the helm. "She's all yours."

Moving in her direction, he plopped down beside her.

"This is amazing." Her smile was big and wide and made her eyes sparkle like the sun on the water.

Suddenly he was more than happy that he'd taken the brothers' challenge. "I hope you're not expecting me to argue with you."

She shook her head at him, then looked over her shoulder and her smile slipped. "Oh, no. They're gaining on us."

He chuckled. "No worries. They still have a lot to learn about racing."

"And your crew knows a lot?"

He nodded. "Oh yeah. My grandfather gave my sister Siobhan a racing boat for her eighteenth birthday and Mick and Tim are the lead crew."

"Your eighteen year old sister races?"

"She grew up on boats, knows as much about sailing as the rest of us, but I think it will be a few more years before she'll crew in an official race." Again, he chuckled. "Though if she has her way, it will be sooner than later."

The boat lilted in the opposite direction and a splash of water washed over the deck and onto them, making Addison squeal again. He was really learning to like those happy shrieks. Actually, he was really learning to like a lot about the beautiful brunette at his side.

"How do we know when we win?" Phone in front of her, she slowly moved from left to right and he realized she was taking a video not photos. Her hands fell to her lap. "Oh, no. They're stopping."

He looked over his shoulder, the Kincaids had fallen far behind and slowed to a near stop. The hardest thing about racing a sailboat was the need for wind, but in this case the wind was still blowing strong. "Looks like they gave up the struggle. This time."

"This time? You know them?"

"The Kincaid boys?" He nodded. "It's a small marina. Everyone knows everyone. Or at least their boats."

"I see." She shifted slightly, slipping her phone back into her small purse. "What happens if there's no wind?"

"We have a motor if the winds won't cooperate or if foul weather creeps up unexpectedly and we need to get out of the way."

"Does that happen often?"

"Sometimes. The key thing is to make sure you always check your gas levels. Last thing you want is to learn the hard way that you've run out of gas."

Her eyes sparkled with amusement. "I'm sure nothing like that has ever happened to you?"

"Moi?" He slapped his palm against his chest and chuckled. "Maybe, but that's a story for another day."

Still smiling at him, she nodded. "So, now what?"

"Up to you. We can stay on the water a little longer. The kitchen below is fully operational. Tim grills some mean shrimp."

"Fresh, of course." She smiled up at him.

He nodded.

"I think I'd like that."

The boat had slowed and continued along the shore at a more leisurely pace. Since the racing boat had no comfortable place to sit on deck, they moved to below deck, where much like an RV, the spaces were versatile. The central area converted to extra sleeping space when needed. Otherwise a good size table and u-shaped booth seating made for a cozy place to eat, or play games, or even work if anyone was foolish enough to spend their time at sea attached to a computer.

It didn't take long for Tim to sauté up something to eat and call for them to go below deck. Kyle stepped aside for her to descend the steps first. At the bottom she stood staring at the set table. "It's a shame we can't bring the fresh air down here too."

He looked to Tim and he shrugged.

"If you don't mind roughing it a bit?" He pointed to the bench cushions. "We could just set those down on the deck."

"A picnic of sorts." She grinned.

"That's about right." Kyle turned to Tim. "You heard the lady."

She walked over to grab a cushion.

"The guys will bring them." Kyle reached for her hand.

"I'm right here." She shook her head at him and grabbed one of the shorter rectangular cushions and handed it to him. "Here you go."

Kyle burst out laughing and accepted the cushion. "Yes, ma'am."

Comfortably on deck, they snacked on the shrimp as well as mussels with fresh toasted garlic bread. Sitting with his legs crossed like a little kid, he munched on the garlic shrimp while she filled him in on her job search.

"I'd rather not move too far from Mom."

"I can understand that."

"But then again." Her gaze lingered off for a moment and he quietly waited for her to finish her thought. "I have to admit there are interviews for positions available that would mean a fast track to higher pay grade, but being too far to drive home for Sunday supper. One opportunity in Midland that's awfully tempting."

In the oil and gas business there were probably multiple

opportunities in West Texas. For all he knew her other options might take her all the way to Alaska. Neither possibility sat well with him. "Have you ever been to the Midland Odessa area?"

She shook her head.

That was one thing in his favor. If she ever interviewed in dry and dusty West Texas, whatever was so tempting might lose its appeal. Then again, if her other choices really were some place breathtaking like Alaska, time to get to know her better was about to run out fast. "But you haven't applied for these positions yet?"

Again, she shook her head.

Baron Enterprises had hotels all over the world. Midland was not one of those places. For a short moment he wondered what the condo market might be like out in the middle of nowhere Texas.

"There's also an opportunity on the East Coast that might be an interesting change of pace. I need to think on it some more."

Good, he liked that. Think on it some more. He'd have to talk to Chase. Find out if there was anything anywhere in Baron Enterprises that would be enticing to an oil and gas engineer and keep her closer to the one spot he often landed. Not that he had a clue what that could be. "What are your plans for tomorrow?"

She shrugged. "Church with Mom in the morning. Then probably digging into my to-be-read pile. Though most likely I'll wind up on the computer looking for more job options."

"Join me for dinner?"

"I don't know that I'm up for any more adventures just yet." She smiled at him then bit into a piece of toast dipped in the garlic butter.

"No adventures. My family does dinner every Sunday at my grandparents' ranch."

"The one near where you drove me off the road."

"Yes. And I truly am sorry about that. I'm usually not such a jerk."

"I know." She blinked at him. "And you've apologized

very nicely for it."

"So I'm forgiven?"

She nodded.

"Excellent. And dinner tomorrow?"

She hesitated, and he knew she was searching for a polite way to say no.

"It's calf season. Do you like baby animals?" Considering she volunteered at the animal shelter, he already knew what her answer would be. He just wasn't so sure if calves held the same appeal to her as kittens.

Her mouth fell open then snapped shut. "Little cows?"

He nodded.

"Oh." Her expression went soft. "How sweet."

Bingo. He'd guessed correctly at making her an offer she couldn't refuse. "Good. Then I'll pick you up at two o'clock."

"But—"

"That will give us plenty of time to see whatever's new in the barn."

She blew out a slow sigh and nodded. "Two o'clock. I'll be ready."

"Great."

He reached for a shrimp and his hand froze midway to his mouth. Until now he'd done everything to keep the women in his life away from his grandfather. What had he just done?

CHAPTER TEN

What was she doing? Addison slipped on her favorite wedge sandals. Comfortable, not too fancy, not too casual. They worked great with a pair of jeans, or a dress. Her Texas upbringing had her rejecting blue jeans for Sunday dinner attire, but she didn't want to overdress either. The sandals had been the easier choice. She had three pairs of Capri pants, two pairs of slacks, and two dresses on her bed to prove that what to wear had been a more challenging choice to make. In the end, she settled for a favorite navy blue sundress with a scoop neck and capped sleeves.

"Don't you look pretty." Her mother put down her knitting and looked up at her daughter. "You really like this young man, don't you?"

She shrugged. What was she supposed to say to her mother. "I suppose."

An engine roared onto the driveway and then cut off. Her mom lifted her head to look out the window. "Well, if nothing else he's punctual. And he has good taste in cars."

"Oh, Mother."

"Hey." Her mom shrugged. "You know what your grandmother always said. It's just as easy to fall in love with a rich man—"

"As a poor man," she finished for her mother, kissed her on the cheek and grabbed her purse. Her mother should know better than to think that the hefty bank account this man, or at least his family, seemed to have would sway her. Love had nothing to do with money. "Don't let your imagination run away with you. I won't be home late."

"Have fun."

Part of her was nervous about dinner with Kyle's family. If they'd been dating longer she might have read something into the invitation, but after only a handful of dates in less than two weeks, the invitation had to be all about the animals. After all, Kyle seemed to be all about having fun, about living. Truly living. This brought a whole new trend of thoughts to mind. What kind of man had all this time and money to spend? Now that she thought about it, she still didn't know what he did for a living. Whatever it was, money didn't seem to be an issue for this family. Maybe she should have dressed up more?

Before he could ring the bell, she yanked the front door open. "Hi."

Kyle flashed a sappy grin at her. "Hi. Ready?"

"Absolutely." She shoved the thought *liar liar pants on fire* to the back of her mind. He picked her up in the same Mercedes he'd run her off the road with. Her mind darted back again to just how much money did these people have? Not that she hadn't figured out they were rich. Probably very rich. After yesterday's excursion on the sailboat she realized very rich was probably a gross understatement, and suddenly this whole dinner idea had her very nervous.

"I should warn you. My grandfather can be a bit…eccentric."

"Eccentric how?" For many people that was a euphemism for batshit crazy. It also could mean somebody who spent all day and night knitting koozies for beer bottles. Once again, Addison had to ask herself what had she gotten herself into.

"My grandfather is no spring chicken and he has grown tired of waiting for great-grandchildren."

Now she had absolutely no idea where he was going with this.

"Lately, he's taken to matching up his grandkids with potential companions that meet his criteria."

"Criteria? And what is that?"

"Heaven only knows, but according to my sister, mostly broad hips. Good for having large families."

Maybe now she was seeing the crazy side of Kyle

instead of the fun side. Or maybe it was the crazy side that fueled the fun side.

"Anyhow, we'll all do our best to protect you from a barrage of questions."

"Like how big are my hips?" she teased.

Kyle chuckled. "Something like that."

"Okay. I don't know what I was expecting, but an overly inquisitive grandfather looking to marry off his grandchildren in search of great-grandchildren, that I can handle."

"Good. Then we're all set."

Taking a turn off the freeway, they wound their way onto a narrow two lane country road just like the one they had met on. For all she knew it was the same road. They'd wandered down this road for only a short distance when he turned on to a dirt road under a large iron arch blazoned with a scrolling letter B. The narrow one lane road twisted through rolling green hills peppered with black cows on either side. It was so hard to believe the family ranch was this close to Houston, and yet a world away.

Coming around the bend, the family home came into view. Right now, she'd bet every penny she had, including her retirement income, that she had just traveled back in time and was approaching Tara from *Gone with the Wind*. "Wow."

"The original house was built by my grandmother's great-grandfather. There have been some additions and updates through the years, but the family has been very protective of the façade."

"I don't have words for this. Stunning comes to mind. Breathtaking is a close second." Most of all, she was realizing that these people had way more money than she had even imagined. Seriously way more.

"It is actually a favorite place for all of us."

"I gather from the cows that it's a working ranch?"

He nodded. "It is."

"So who's the rancher?"

This time Kyle chuckled. "Technically, none of us, but we all could be if we had to. At any given time you'll see one of us or my cousins on a horse, or in the barn, or riding the fence line, fixing posts, or whatever needs to be done."

She tipped her head to the side and closed one eye, staring at him. It was easy to picture him in jeans with a button down shirt and the heroic white Stetson on his head.

The road formed a circle in front of the house. Kyle came to a stop by the massive double front doors and on cue, an older gentleman hurried down the front steps with a much younger man on his heels. "Miss Eve and Mr. Craig are waiting for you inside. The Senator is in the barn."

"And the Governor?"

The man shook his head. "The annual fundraising committee had a meeting after church. Your grandparents should be home shortly."

Following Kyle up the steps, two words were rattling around in Addison's head. Senator and Governor. One political nickname maybe, but two? The front hall felt as big as her apartment. To her left a pretty brunette looked up from a sofa in the front parlor. Pushing to his feet, a man with hair a shade too dark to be called blonde and piercing green eyes seemed to hide a world of hurt, smiled at her. As she moved closer, it struck her like a bolt of lightening. Kyle was a member of *the* Baron family. Holy moly. Now what?

All the color unexpectedly drained from Addison's face. Kyle didn't know if she needed a fan, a chair, or a stiff drink.

"You're a Baron?"

He nodded, wondering what was she aiming for.

"Your grandfather is former Governor Baron." This time it wasn't a question.

He nodded again, only now he understood. She was only now connecting the dots of his name and his family.

"I think I'm going to faint."

Unsure if she was serious or exaggerating, he opted not

to take a chance, and put his arm around her waist.

His sister cast a sideways glance at him.

"I think she can use some water." He guided her toward the nearest chair; his brother Craig walked briskly to the bar and poured her a glass.

Eve pushed him aside and guided Addison the last few steps to the most comfortable chair in the room. "Here you go."

With Addison comfortably settled in their grandfather's recliner, Eve accepted the glass her brother held out for her and took a short sip. "Thank you."

"You're really going to have to learn to slow the heck down," Eve barked at Kyle. "Not everyone is meant to break the sound barrier."

"For your information," Kyle waved a finger at his sister, "I drove the speed limit."

"No one in Texas actually drives the speed limit." Craig took a sip of his own drink.

"Well, I did." He wasn't going to add that he hadn't been in a hurry to get to the family home. Not so much that he wanted to delay the inevitable, as much as he simply wanted to spend more time alone with Addison.

"Please don't argue on my account." Addison swallowed one more sip of her water. "I'm fine. It was not Kyle's driving that threw me for a loop."

Craig stood up. "Should I get you something stronger?"

She smiled up at the brother. "No, thank you. I'm okay now."

The plan for the afternoon had been to visit with his siblings for a little while, before the Governor and his grandmother arrived. Help Addison feel comfortable before facing down the family matchmaker. Visiting the barn had been on his agenda for after dinner, but now he was thinking a little baby animal therapy might be in order. "What do you say we hit the barn and visit the animals?"

Even though most of the color had returned to her face already, it was the suggestion of visiting the animals that brought a smile to her face. "That would be very nice. If nobody minds."

Eve smiled at the two. "Mitch is at the barn. We have another rejected calf. He's trying to get one of the mothers who lost her calf to accept the orphaned one."

"If anyone can do it, he can." Kyle nodded and extended his hand to Addison.

Very hesitantly, she accepted the proffered hand and if he wasn't mistaken, when her fingers linked with his he thought he could actually feel her tension easing away. He liked the idea that maybe being with him made a difference, made things better. Of course he was probably projecting his own feelings on her. Just because having her hand in his made his whole world brighter didn't mean she felt the same way.

Instead of taking her through the house and out the back door, he opted for the shorter distance to the front door. The walk around the house to the barn would be warmer and longer, but his instincts told him exposing her to the large home at this particular moment wasn't in his or her best interest.

Out the front door, Kyle slowed his pace to match hers. They'd made it half way around the house when he final dared to say something. "Fresh air helps, doesn't it?"

She nodded and took a few more steps before slowing her gait and glancing up at him. "Your family is the closest thing to royalty after the Kennedy's."

"Just don't say that in front of my grandfather." The Baron family was often referred to that way. The Governor made it perfectly clear that while he couldn't deny money had its privilege in this and any other country, he disliked being referred to as royalty. Still, if pressed on the subject, he would huff that the Baron's of Texas didn't come after any one. "He would vehemently disagree."

"With which part?"

Kyle laughed. "All of it."

"You're trying to tell me he's down to earth?"

"He's a former Marine, down to earth isn't in his vocabulary."

His words brought a short bubble of laughter from her.

"Here we are." He gestured to the large open doorway

with his free arm.

"Looks like every picture of a barn I've ever seen." Her gaze lifted to the high ceilings, down to the hay strands scattered about the floor, over to the bales of hay stacked high in a corner, the loft above, and then left to right at the stall doors on either side. "Somehow it still seems much bigger than what I expected."

"Even though the Governor went into politics after leaving the corps, Cedar Ridge has always been a working ranch and as the family grows, so has the operation."

"And to this day none of you work the ranch?" Her head continued to rotate around, taking in her surroundings.

He shook his head. "There's a foreman, lots of hands. As kids we thought Mitch would grow up and take part in the ranch, but after graduating from A&M he joined the military."

"Marines?"

"Nope. Air Force. Learned to fly planes. Did that until he started to struggle with night blindness. Next thing we knew he ran for state senator and won. Two years after that he was tapped to fill the shoes of a retiring US senator."

Halfway down the length of the barn, his brother the senator, glanced up in their direction. His expression blank until he focused on Addison. One eyebrow subtly rose for a brief instant before the poker face descended again. "Giving a tour?"

"Sort of." Kyle slapped his brother on the back. "How's it going?"

Finally a hint of a smile appeared on the senator's face. "Good. I think it's going to work. Surrogate mom seems happy."

"Does this happen often?" Addison asked, her eyes lasering in on the calf now wobbling away from the new mama cow over to where they stood at the rails.

"Rejected calves? Too often." Kyle squatted down and spread his fingers in front of the calf.

"And matching them up with a different mama cow?"

Kyle lifted his eyes to his brother in silent communication that this was his territory.

"Doesn't work as often as we'd like. Sometimes we simply have no choice but to hand feed a rejected or orphaned calf." Mitch squatted beside his brother and scratching the edge of the small animal's jaw, smiled when the calf leaned away from Kyle and pushed his head into the palm of Mitch's hand. "This is a sweet one."

Addison squatted beside the two men and grinned. "Wow. Look at those eyes."

"Soulful," Mitch said softly.

"Now I understand the cliché about making cow eyes. So big and brown and almost mesmerizing." When the calf took a step forward and pressed against her, knocking her onto her rear, she giggled. When the little guy nudged against her face, she chuckled more loudly, but when he tried to curl up in her lap, she nearly fell over laughing. "You are way too big for a lap dog, sweetie."

Mitch's eyes rounded with surprise. "I think you've made a friend."

"I guess so." She shifted, encouraging the little guy to lie down beside her instead of on her. All the while she scratched the side of the animal's jaw the same as Mitch had moments ago.

Again, his brother's eyes gave silent insight to the complicated man. Kyle could tell Mitch was impressed with Addison's instinctive responses to the new calf. When Mitch's gaze lifted to meet his, he could read his brother telling him exactly what he was starting to think in this short time: this one's a keeper.

CHAPTER ELEVEN

By the time Addison left the barn, she'd been considerably more relaxed than when she'd first spotted the massive house atop the rolling hills. Halfway through dinner she'd concluded that she had to be dreaming, sitting at a massive table, surrounded by one of the country's most prominent and recognizable families— even if it had taken her the better part of two weeks to connect the dots. Except this wasn't a dream. She knew because she'd continuously pinched herself through the meal. Though the more startling thing was just how normal everyone seemed. Somewhere in the back of her mind she remembered thinking during the elections a few years ago that Mitchell Baron would be a good choice for the job, but why she'd thought that eluded her. Now she was happy to see her first impressions of a nice guy wanting to do good for his state had not been wrong. At this table, surprisingly enough, there were no egos, no extravagances—unless you counted all the forks and the linen tablecloth on the table— even the intimidating Governor seemed like any ordinary old man who still happened to appreciate his wife.

As a matter of fact, she'd say the man adored his wife. That made her smile. Her own dad had passed away when she was pretty young. Her memories of her parents together were few and far between. She liked how every so often the Governor would lock gazes with his wife across the table and smile. After all the years together they were still as smitten as a pair of young lovers. And they were Barons. Everyone at the table was a prominent member of the business world. A CEO, a senator, a movie mogul, the list was long. On that list was Kyle's chosen profession. This of course had her kicking herself for not having realized she'd been spending time with a world famous race car driver.

"How much longer?" Sitting to his left was Kyle's brother, Chase. Addison had learned that his wife CJ was visiting her sister in Hollywood for a girl's weekend so he'd driven down from Dallas for the family dinner.

Addison had done plenty of laughing over the appetizers and the story of Chase hiring a date for their cousin's wedding. It gave yesterday's conversation with Kyle about a matchmaking grandfather a bit more perspective.

"I've actually got a doctor's appointment tomorrow." Kyle wiggled the fingers on his injured hand. "Will know then if this thing is healing the way it's supposed to or if I'm going to have a longer haul."

"So you might be able to drive the Austin race?" Eve asked.

He shrugged. "Maybe. Either way I'm going to head over to the track so I can check out how Gibs is doing."

"That's the back up driver, right?" Craig lifted his gaze from the dish in front of him.

"That's right."

"I haven't heard much either way." Eve took a sip of her water. "Then again, I haven't been watching the races since you're not driving."

"I thought you didn't watch my races." The serious words took on a playful tone.

"I don't." She took another sip, her eyes twinkling with mischief, she bit back a smile. "Usually."

"Right." Still grinning, Kyle bobbed his head at his sister.

Following the conversation was challenging at times, hilarious at others. Shortly after his sister's comment, Kyle leaned into Addison and softly explained that for years his sister had reminded him what a dangerous job he had and how nerve wracking it was for her and a handful of other family members like their mother and grandmother.

"How did you get into racing?" Addison asked softly.

"That would be our mother's fault." Eve leaned back in

her chair. "After the divorce, Mom would spend all school breaks in Belgium."

Kyle nodded. "Near Spa."

Her expression must have shown her challenge connecting the dot.

"Formula One hot spot," Craig volunteered. "Drivers start training young and we were in the right place at the right time for Speed Racer here to catch the bug."

"Belgium?" she repeated.

"Once the youngest graduated high school, Mom settled permanently in Belgium." Kyle chuckled. "She said it was more civilized."

"Rather ironic that Mom's efforts to find peace and tranquility has caused her continual anxiety during the racing season." Craig took a sip of water and turned to his grandfather. "You two are being awfully quiet."

Mrs. Baron casually shrugged. "It is what it is."

Her response made the Governor smile, and Mitch at her other side leaned in her direction and spoke very softly. "One of the Governor's favorite expressions."

Addison bobbed her head in understanding just as Kyle leaned into her other side. "Anyone who survived a lifetime of waiting for her husband to come home from war after war can handle a perfectly safe once a week race."

Until now, Addison had thought Kyle was a perfectly nice and charming adrenaline junkie. After that last statement she was thinking the man was actually rather delusional. How could he expect anyone to believe driving at 200 miles per hour was perfectly safe?

"You don't look convinced." Her point made, Eve slowly cut into the last two bites of her meal giving her brother some food for thought.

Addison had thought she was hiding her thoughts well, especially since she was totally out of her element, but Eve had gotten very good at reading her. Though it shouldn't come as a surprise. Everything Kyle had told her about his siblings made it clear that he cared very deeply for all of them. It was also pretty clear that he truly believed Eve was actually the smartest sibling. Addison could see why he thought so.

Another hour of everyone chatting at the table before moving outside to the patio and Addison was impressed by how normal it all felt. Despite the trappings, they really were just nice people. Almost too nice. No one excused themselves, no one looked bored, no one seemed in a hurry to go home. She almost felt guilty that she needed Kyle to drive her home.

"Ready?" He pushed away from his chair.

She looked left then right. Had she said something out loud? No one else seemed to be reacting to her thoughts. Only Kyle.

"You mentioned you wanted to get home early to your mom."

That's right. She had. Still, the fact that he explained his response right when she was questioning her own thoughts made her wonder. The family might be a bit too nice, but could Kyle be too perfect?

The long ride home to Addison's mother's house passed by so quickly Kyle almost flew past the exit. All sorts of images came to mind as he and Addison chatted in the car. A flash of the picture of her sitting on the floor playing with the calf made him smile. She really is an amazing woman, but it was time she see a little more of his world. "Do you have any plans for later this week?"

"You mean besides interviewing?"

"You have an interview lined up?" He didn't mean to sound so surprised.

"Not yet, but I'm hopeful that Monday morning someone will notice what an amazing person I am and that their business can't survive without me. Or at least without interviewing me."

That made Kyle laugh.

Driving down her mother's narrow street, he pulled into the driveway. Addison unbuckled her seatbelt and faced him. "I really did have a lovely time. Well," she grinned, "once I got over being nervous about your family. They really are just like everyone else. And your grandfather is kind of cute."

"Cute?" He'd heard the Governor described in many ways but cute had never been one of them.

"I suppose he can appear gruff to many people, but he has such deep blue smiling eyes."

"Smiling eyes?" Now he was starting to wonder about Addison's sanity.

"Don't look so surprised. His demeanor is sweet even though his voice sounds somewhat stern."

"Somewhat?"

"Okay, so the man has a very stern disposition. He's a powerful man with a disciplined history." She waved a finger at him and smiled a grin that seemed to say she had the biggest secret in the world. "But look deep into his eyes. When he was talking about any of you, even though his words might have appeared harsh or gruff, the love that sparkled in his eyes was evident to anyone who looked."

At this particular moment in time, whether she was the most observant person in the world or completely out of her mind, he wasn't sure. Every single one of his siblings and cousins knew that their grandfather not only loved them, he would risk his life for them without batting an eye or a moment's hesitation, but smiling eyes? He was going to have to pay more attention.

Hurrying around the car, Kyle reached the passenger door just as she stepped out. Extending his hand, she linked fingers with his and stood upright. "Thanks."

Even though convention said it was time to let go of her hand, he opted to keep a hold on her. Delighted when she made no effort to retrieve her hand. Not until they climbed the steps onto the front porch, and she needed both hands to retrieve her keys and unlocked the door, did he let go.

Key in the lock, she turned the latch and shoved the door open. Expecting her to step inside, he took a short step forward only to have her retreat a step and turn to face him, smashing herself against his chest. The sudden impact had her momentarily losing her balance. A man used to relying on his reflexes, he quickly manacled her upper arms in his hold to help steady her.

"Sorry," she muttered softly. Her weight shifted back but with his hold on her, she couldn't move.

He knew he should let go, let her into the house, but all he could do was stare into her eyes. The deep brown eyes with little flecks of gold drew him in like a red dot mesmerized a fickle feline. Instead of easing away, he leaned forward. "Addison?"

"Hmm," she mumbled, her gaze locked on his, her lips barely parting to release the sound.

Resistance was futile. He needed to kiss her as much as he needed the air in his next breath. Daring to lower his head another few inches, he was rewarded with her face tipping upward. Only a breath away from tasting heaven, his mouth carefully dared to touch hers.

"Addison, honey. Is that you?" The sound of her mother's voice on the other side of the half open door reached them two seconds before the door swung fully open and they each sprang backward like a couple of kids caught with their hands in the proverbial cookie jar.

"I, uh, better get back to the ranch." It took every ounce of determination he had to step away from the door and away from Addison. "Let me know how many companies see the light."

Addison's stunned expression shifted to a sly grin. "I'll do that."

There were a lot of things he was sure of and that she would be an asset beyond measure to any company was most definitely one of them. That he wished her mother had waited just a few more minutes to notice them on the porch was another.

CHAPTER TWELVE

"**L**ooks to me like things are going well with your new friend." Addison's mom didn't bother looking up from her knitting. From where Addison sat, she could see the corners of her mother's mouth tipping upward in the slightest of smiles. The woman never was very good at hiding her thoughts or feelings. It was pretty obvious to Addison that her mom was enjoying the moment.

Not since she was a teenager had her mom caught her in an almost compromising position and the whole thing felt really… odd. Not just that her mother interrupted what she was sure would have been an amazing kiss, but the entire friendship with a member of a prominent and socially elite family. She was so seriously out of her league in so many ways.

"Cat got your tongue?" Her mom's grin widened just a smidge.

Addison sucked in a deep breath. Sooner or later her mother would need to know more about Kyle. Even if they remained only friends, she couldn't keep who he was a secret forever. "I'm not sure."

This time her mom's hand stilled, and her gaze lifted to meet her daughter's. "Care to clarify?"

"You already know that I think he's a nice guy."

Her mother nodded.

"And you know that I've never had so much fun spending time with a man." She paused gathering her thoughts, considering her words, and trying very hard not to smile like the village idiot while thinking about how energized she was whenever she spent time with Kyle. Of course, racing around in go-karts, beating him at putt putt golf, and racing a sailboat probably had as much to do with it as how easy it felt to be around him. "You also know he's a bit of an adrenaline junkie."

Still silent, her mother's eyes widened just enough to see the whites of her eyes circle wide.

"I mean, how often does the average person get to race sailboats?"

Her casual smile returning, Addison's mom blew out a soft breath. "I admit, I'm a little envious."

"What?"

"You know that old song about life carrying on even after the thrill of living is gone?"

Addison nodded. It was one of many golden oldies she'd grown up singing alongside her mother.

"Your young man reminds me of your father. He always enjoyed life to the last drop. I didn't realize how much I missed that until the past couple of weeks watching you."

"Oh, Mom."

Her mother's hand went up in the air, palm out. "Don't make a big deal of it. This is how aging is supposed to work, what we can't do ourselves, we do vicariously through our kids. And some day," her mother's grin widened, "through our grandchildren."

"Now you sound like the Governor."

"Governor?" Confusion settled between her mom's brows.

"Yeah." This was it. Time to spill the beans. "Turns out the reason that Kyle has access to so many cars, and boats, and a big ranch is because he's a Baron."

Her mother stared intently, then she finally shook her head. Her mouth opened to speak when suddenly her eyes widened and her jaw dropped ever so slightly before snapping shut. "As in former Governor James Baron?"

"That would be Kyle's grandfather.

"Wow." Her mom set her knitting down and leaned back. "My baby is dating a Baron."

She almost nodded when it struck her, was she really

dating him or was she just an intermittent distraction? Something to do until he returned to the racing circuit? "That may be an overstatement."

Her mother shrugged. "Didn't look that way to me."

Didn't feel that way to her either, but what did she know about running around with the rich and famous. As far as she was concerned, the Barons were pretty much the richest and most famous family in Texas, right up there with Ross Perot and the King Ranch. "He's recovering from a broken wrist. He can't race until it heals. Something about needing to be able to unbuckle himself in five seconds. He can't get behind the wheel of a race car until he can do that."

"Race car." Her mom inched forward in her seat. "My sweet, sensible, pencil pushing, engineer of a daughter is dating a race car driver?"

"Like I said, dating may be an over-statement."

"Uh huh." Her mother sank back into her favorite chair. "You keep telling yourself that. Oh." She snapped her fingers. "You got a call earlier today from one of those headhunters you're using."

"On a Sunday?"

Her mom shrugged. "She said to call her when you have a chance. Something about securing an interview for a position with the State Department. Any position in particular?"

"Analyst at the Bureau of Intelligence and Research."

"Intelligence? Isn't that a euphemism for the CIA?"

"You've been watching too much TV."

"I don't think so." Her mother picked up her knitting again. "Imagine that. My quietly brilliant engineer is going to be a spy."

"I am not going to be a spy." Who knew her mother could have such a vivid imagination. "I simply thought it might be a good time for a career shift."

"That would be quite a shift. I don't suppose your new fella has anything to do with this unexpected sense of employment adventure."

"Of course not." At least she didn't think so.

"By any chance is there a State Department branch office in Texas?"

She almost sighed out loud. Of course her mother would expect her to only consider the safe and secure jobs close to home. Except, ever since meeting Kyle, she'd begun to realize that not only did she work too hard, her life was, well, boring and maybe it was time to grab the brass ring and make some changes. Only now that she had spent so much time with Kyle, relocating to the East Coast didn't hold as much appeal as it should. Or maybe her brains might have been scrambled after a day at the go-kart track. Or maybe it was Kyle that was doing all the scrambling.

Shoving the front door of the family home open, Kyle hadn't expected to almost crash into his brother Chase.

"You're home earlier than I expected."

He turned his wrist to look at his watch. "I told you I wouldn't be long."

"Right." His brother grinned at him.

"It's not like that."

Chase slapped his brother on the back of his shoulder and shook his head. "I have to head out. Maybe some other time you can explain to me how seeing the same woman more than once, never mind several times, *and* bringing her home for dinner, isn't different."

Before Kyle could say another word, his brother was out the door and bounding down the front steps.

"Well, isn't this a pleasant surprise." His sister came up the hall, a drink in each hand.

"Not you too." He tipped his chin in the direction of her hands. "And since when have you become a two-fisted drinker?"

Eve chuckled and did a ninety degree turn toward the library. "First of all, your wicked ways have not worn off on me, these are merely sweet teas. One for me and one for Grams. And not me too what?"

"Never mind. Everyone in the library?"

"Just about everyone has gone home. It's just the grandparents and me, and now you." She crossed into the room where their grandparents sat side by side on the loveseat. Somehow that seemed oddly more appropriate than sitting on an ordinary sofa not designed for lovebirds.

"We didn't expect to see you back so soon." His grandfather met his gaze. "I like that girl. Good hips."

"James." His grandmother elbowed her husband.

"What? It's true."

Lila Baron shook her head. "That may be so, but it doesn't need to be vocalized."

"Of course, dear." The Governor patted his wife's hand and then returned his attention to Kyle. "For what it's worth, she's sensible too. It wouldn't do you any harm to think about settling down."

It took a great deal of discipline not to roll his eyes at his grandfather. That man had settling down and breeding on the brain and it wasn't fun for any of his grandchildren. "Yes, sir."

The old man's brows knit together as he studied his grandson's rapid response. At times like this when their grandfather focused on them so intently, all the kids felt as if the man could not only read their minds but their souls too. Probably why they so often broke down and confessed to whatever misdeed had earned that look without the man needing to say a single word.

"Then you're thinking you can't live on the edge forever?"

Dang it. Maybe the man really could read minds. Perhaps not so much about his on the edge lifestyle, but at least about his career. He wasn't getting any younger, and unlike the octogenarian musicians still performing to sell out crowds, like pro football, racing took a toll on a man. Something he'd avoided thinking about, until recently. Very recently. Till Addison recently. Suddenly, he might have found a reason to be more careful. About a lot of things. "Maybe."

"Maybe?" Eve looked up, and much like her

grandfather had just done, she stared him down as if trying to read his soul. Glancing away, she shook her head. "Nope. Not buying it. The only way you'll ever slow down is when you're six feet under. And even then I wouldn't put it past you to climb out from the grave at two hundred miles per hour."

The Governor took a sip of his brandy. "Two fifty."

From her spot next to her husband, Lila Baron bit back a smile at her husband's attempt at a joke at her grandson's expense. Then, meeting Kyle's gaze, she mouthed *I love you*. Just as quickly, Kyle mouthed back, *I love you more*. Sure of their grandmother's endless unconditional love, the love-you-mores and love-you-bests were a longstanding family tradition.

"Shall I have Hazel bring you a tea too?" Eve cut off the love fest.

"Or join me in a brandy?" the Governor asked.

"I think I'll take the brandy." The kind of thoughts Kyle was grappling to accept required something with a little more aging and a lot less sugar.

"Well," Grams pushed to her feet, "I'm going to call it a night."

"Yes." The Governor stood as well. "Early to bed, early to rise."

Hugs and kisses and good-nights were shared.

The moment the sound of their grandparents' footsteps faded down the hall, Eve turned her attention to her brother. "You seriously thinking about slowing down or just playing lip service to the old man?"

"Eventually everyone thinks of slowing down. We all have to face our own mortality some day."

"I'm sorry." She put her glass down and leaned forward in the seat. "Did my adrenaline junkie brother, the man who never met a risk he didn't want to take, just use the words 'slow down' and 'mortality' in the same sentence?"

"Maybe?"

"Oh, you are throwing that word around a whole lot tonight."

It suddenly struck him, why was his sister the last one

left. "How come you're still here?"

She shook her head. "No dropping chaff allowed."

"We can talk about my momentary lapse of judgment some other time. Why *are* you still here?"

Taking a slow sip, she hefted a lazy shoulder. "Didn't feel like making the drive back to Houston."

"And?"

"No and." She took another sip.

"Right. And?"

"Jack said he was going to stop by my townhouse tonight if we got done with supper early. I think somewhere in all our casual plus ones, I may have sent the wrong message."

As much as he'd rather not know anything about some of the private aspects of his sister's life, he was most definitely relieved that she didn't have any romantic interest in his long-time friend. A man who made Kyle look like a risk averse monk. "Want me to have a talk with him?"

She shook her head. "No, I will. But I knew I wouldn't be up to it after a dinner with this crowd. Besides, I hate to lie."

That made him smile. As a kid, if a rule was broken she was always the first one to give the culprit up. Not that she was a tattler, but if confronted, she really couldn't lie. "It'll be nice to have company over coffee in the morning."

"What? You don't think I'm going to rise with the chickens and the Governor?" Her valiant effort to keep a straight face failed as she almost spit tea at him from snickering.

"Says the pot to the kettle. Whoever is up first, rap on the other's door."

"Deal." She nodded and set her glass on the desktop. "I think I'll call it an early night."

"See you in the morning."

She leaned in and kissed his cheek as she walked past him. "Goodnight."

Settling into his grandfather's desk chair, he glanced over at the brandy bottle on the bar. It wasn't really his favorite. He'd said yes more to share with the Governor than for the taste of it. Holding his cell phone, he tapped at recent photos, enlarging the photo he'd snapped of Addison holding onto the sailboat's lifeline for all she was worth, and then another with her laughing from deep inside only a few hours later. He couldn't afford to let someone into his heart. It wouldn't be fair to her. And yet, like it or not, she'd already made herself at home deep in his heart and soul.

CHAPTER THIRTEEN

The last few days had kept Kyle busy making arrangements. He'd intentionally limited his interactions with Addison to phone calls and kept those short as well. After spending a long night tossing and turning, chasing sleep, unable to get visions of Addison out of his head, he decided it was time to fish or cut bait. So to speak.

After a mere twenty-four hours he realized cutting bait was not an option. There was no keeping Addison out of his thoughts and there was no getting a good night's rest. Not until he'd decided that if they had any possibility of a future together, she'd have to see what his world was really like, and that had taken just about every minute of time to organize.

"You look awfully pensive." A basket of fresh cut flowers on her arm, his grandmother came in the back door.

"Just working out a few things."

Lila Baron nodded. "Yes, I can see that." She came up behind him at the kitchen table and laid a hand on his shoulders. "Just don't think too much, affairs of the heart are best handled by the heart not the brain."

He placed his hand over hers and looking up over his shoulder, he smiled at her. "Thank you."

Another curt nod and loving smile and his grandmother settled by the kitchen sink, pruning and trimming and creating what he knew would become lovely floral arrangements placed throughout the house.

His phone sounded and tapping the sheet of paper in front of him, he took the call.

"It's all set." His manager Gilbert didn't bother with

polite preambles.

"Thanks."

"Next time give me more warning."

If things went the way he hoped, there wouldn't be a need for a next time. "They're expecting us?"

"Yes, and the safety car is at your disposal as well."

"Great. Thanks." In his mind he'd worked out all the details and knew that Gilbert would pull it all together, but it was still a relief to see it all coming together. "I've got to run if we're going to get there in time to catch the practice."

"Any updates on how long before you can return to the team?"

Even though his manager couldn't see him, he shrugged. "My six weeks are up. I'm cleared for normal life. I'll know by the end of day if it will be soon or not."

"I've waited this long, I suppose I can wait a few more hours."

"Attaboy." A few more words and Kyle cut off the call. He had to boogie to get Addison. His normally low heart rate had kicked up a notch. Anyone would think he was a young teen picking up the prom queen. If this idea went south, he didn't know what he was going to do.

Addison shouldn't have been surprised at how well the man could keep a secret. Once again she had no idea where they were going, or what they would be doing. All he had told her was to wear comfortable clothes and shoes. Pants preferred.

All sorts of ideas rattled around in her head. Torn between anticipation, excitement, and potentially sheer terror, she really didn't have a clue what his plans were. The only thing she could do was to pray he didn't expect her to do something insane, like jump out of an airplane.

When they pulled up to a guard shack at the entrance to a massive parking lot for an arena or stadium of some kind, she was at least able to discard sky diving as his little surprise. "If you brought me here to play baseball or football, you're sheer out of luck. Not a coordinated bone in my body."

He let out a strong cackle and pulled into a space by other cars and a main entrance. "Don't buy that for a minute from the lady who caught onto balancing herself on a racing sailboat in only a few hours."

"That's different. Balance won't help me swing and hit a ball or catch it."

"Perhaps."

She stepped out of the car, delighted when he stretched out his arm and curled her hand in his, then slowly, pulled her into the fold of his arms. His gaze settled on hers, his arms hung loosely around her waist, and before she could fully process what was happening, his lips came down to barely touch hers. When he eased back, she almost fell forward against him, yearning for more.

"I needed to do that before we go inside. Just in case."

"In case of what?"

"You'll see." He tugged on her hand and in only a few minutes she realized they weren't at a ballpark but a racetrack.

"Is this where you race?"

He shook his head. "No. I race all over the country and world. The cars and the rules are different for me."

"How so?"

"For one thing, we race in teams of two cars."

"That makes no sense. I mean, let's assume you and your teammate are in first and second place. Wouldn't that mean you're competing not as a team but against each other?"

He chuckled. "Sort of. But we do whatever is necessary for the good of the team."

"I see." At least she sort of understood. What she really didn't see was why they were here.

"Hey man." A tall gentleman in his mid-forties, give or take a few years, approached them, broad grin on his face, hand extended.

Kyle pulled him into a back-slapping hug. "I really

appreciate you working with Gilbert to make this happen."

Taking hold of her hand again, Kyle followed his friend through the building and down to what she assumed was the heart of the track. The very loud heart of the track.

"You'll want to see this." His friend waved a finger at the track. "Got one of our newer back ups about to take a test run."

"How's he been doing?"

"Not bad. His timing isn't there yet."

She took a seat in the bleachers beside him. The two men spoke racing, but she focused on the car taking laps. The young driver had gone around the track several times, another car beating him every time.

"What do you think?" Kyle shifted his attention from the friend on his other side, to her.

"He's braking too early."

"Really?" Kyle smiled, but his friend leaned forward to better see her.

"Yeah. If you watch both cars, you'll see the one who's making better time waits to brake. Your friend, on the other hand, seems to brake about 30 meters before his opponent."

Kyle turned his head slightly toward his friend.

His friend smiled and bobbed his head. "You got all that after watching a couple of laps?"

"It's basic math."

"She's an engineer," Kyle explained.

The friend nodded again. "Notice anything else?"

"Well. I'm sure if I studied the laps more closely I might come up with some other observations, but for now it's the braking too early and then he should throttle earlier. As soon as he's out of the apex of the turn, he should hit the throttle, then he'd take off faster."

"And you figured all this out after watching him race for a few minutes?" The friend's tone didn't make it clear if he was impressed by her or making fun of her.

"She's smart." Kyle grinned as if he'd invented a better wheel all by himself.

Now she didn't care how the other guy meant his comment. The pride in Kyle's eyes was all she needed to feel like a winner. She was in so much trouble where Kyle was involved. If she wasn't in love with him already, she was dang well on her way.

Kyle couldn't be more proud of Addison if she'd single handedly found a cure for cancer. "You ready for your surprise?"

"There's more?"

He nodded and stood up. "Come with me."

"I'll catch you later." His friend slapped him on the shoulder.

Starting to feel the energy of the track, she was actually looking forward to whatever he wanted to show her now. Down near the wide track surrounded by grass, signage, and plenty of buzz from cars and people, she found herself in a garage with a handful of people wandering about and one really sleek car. In lime green.

"Hey, Kyle." Another man in coveralls and carrying a stack of folded cloth, appeared. "You ready?"

He nodded and accepted the pile of what she now realized were more coveralls. Kyle spun about and handed her a pair off the top, then pointed over her shoulder. "There's a restroom straight back there. Just slip these on over your clothes."

She didn't need a mirror to be sure that her expression probably resembled a startled owl with its mouth wide open. Snapping it shut, she stared down at the clothing in her hands, then glanced up at him. "Say again?"

"If we're going for a ride, you'll need to wear the protective gear."

Now she looked at the neon colored car and back. "I'm not driving that thing."

"No, you're not."

Relieved, she exhaled deeply. "Good."

"I am." Kyle smiled. "You'll be in the passenger seat."

Panic threatened to bring her lunch up. "I don't think so."

"I promise I won't go too fast."

Like beauty, too fast was most likely in the eyes—or opinions—of the beholder. "I don't think so."

"I find that what I do is less frightening for people if they understand it's safer than they think."

There was no need for a degree in engineering to understand that velocity and mass could easily equal deadly force. "I really don't think that's necessary."

"So, if I were to drive full speed around the track right now, you'd be perfectly calm watching?"

She came within an inch of nodding yes, when she realized that deadly force was deadly force whether or not she was in the car, and sighed. "Maybe not."

"I see." He lowered his head and the sparkle in his eyes dimmed.

Why did he have to look like a little kid whose favorite candy fell on the floor? And why did she feel so compelled to bring the sparkle back? "You promise to go slow?"

He shuffled his feet, and rubbed the back of his neck with one hand. "I believe I said I won't go fast."

"Isn't not fast the definition of slow?" Already she was regretting saying anything.

His head shook from side to side. "No, fast is not fast, slow is boring."

Heaven help her. She supposed this was better than jumping out of an airplane. Maybe. "Okay, but if we die, I promise to find you in heaven and make your life a living hell."

A huge grin spread across his face.

"What is so funny?"

"You think I'm going to heaven?"

"Men!" She spun about and stomped to the less than pristine restroom. A few minutes later, Kyle and his friend were outfitting her with bootie-like shoe coverings, gloves, a neck guard, and helmet. She felt like an alien. The kind from outer space.

Sitting in the car, she reached for the safety harness and strapped herself in. Taking a second to look at her surroundings, it struck her that the inside of the car seemed awfully bare bones. "Is this thing really safe?"

"Very. This is nothing like the cars I drive. This is a two passenger safety car that is often used for special trainings, or demonstrations like we're about to do. But, just so you know, through the years they've continued to improve automobile safety for racers."

She nodded her head. Not truly convinced, but she wasn't going to let her mind get stuck on that bone.

"For our little foray we'll be the only car on the track."

That actually made her feel a little better—not good, but better. Slowly he pulled away from the garage and she sucked in a long breath. When they reached the track, he eased on and as he'd promised, didn't drive too fast. As a matter of fact, she probably drove faster on I45 going between her condo in Houston and her mom's place. Maybe this wasn't such a bad idea.

"You doing okay?" he asked without looking at her.

She nodded. "Yeah, I am."

"Trust me?"

"I think so."

"Only think?"

It took her a second to let her thoughts and feelings mingle and evolve. To her surprise, realization slapped her in the face. Despite being strapped into a specialty race car, she actually did trust him. Completely. "I do."

"Good. Then hang on."

The car took off, somewhere between driving on the local freeway and warp speed on the Enterprise. And yet, she wasn't looking for a grab handle, or slamming her foot on a non-existent brake. She was simply along for the ride, and taking it better than she would have thought. By the time he'd done a few laps and rolled into the pit, she actually felt disappointment that the ride was over.

It suddenly struck her that career change or not, life would be terribly boring once Kyle returned to racing and traveling the world—without her.

He hopped out of the car and two men came running to help her. Once her helmet was off, she spun around to find Kyle at her side. "What do you think?"

"Can we do it again?"

His head snapped back and a roar of laughter escaped. "We can't today, but we will. I promise."

Without thinking, she threw her arms around his neck and in front of God and the racing world, she gave him a hard kiss smack on the lips.

When one of the guys who helped her cleared his throat loudly, they pulled apart, and smiling, Kyle's gaze met hers. "Definitely going to do that again, and very soon."

CHAPTER FOURTEEN

The day at the track couldn't have gone any better. Kyle had known that it was the make it or break it moment. Now he'd spent the last few days kicking around what to do next. Few drivers continued on the circuit after their mid thirties. He wasn't ready to retire. Those who didn't want to let go switched to the slower Indy cars. He wasn't sure yet if that was the path he wanted to take. He wasn't sure of much of anything any more.

"You look perplexed." His grandfather looked up from the book he'd been reading in his favorite chair.

"Just thinking."

"Change isn't always easy, but it helps when it comes about for a good reason." The older man slipped a paper bookmark into place, closed the book, and set it on the side table. "When are you seeing that nice young lady again?"

"As a matter of fact, I'm on my way to pick her up now. We're going to dinner."

"Why don't you bring her here for dinner?" His grandmother paused her knitting. "Last time we didn't have much chance to get to know her with so much family here. We'd love to have her back."

"I don't know—" Kyle started to say.

"Excellent idea as always, dear." The Governor turned to his grandson. "You won't want to disappoint your grandmother, will you?"

"No, sir." Though he was positive the disappointment had nothing to do with his grandmother and everything to do with his grandfather's interest in great-grandchildren. An interest he was beginning to share with the old man. And wasn't that the last thing he'd expected to happen to him.

The drive to the animal shelter where Addison volunteered felt shorter than usual. Despite his tendency for a lead foot on the freeway, he'd kept it at the speed limit, but his own thoughts had him so preoccupied, he'd almost missed the exit. Inside, he was once again greeted by the bouncing puppies in the small corral. Only they were down to just two pups.

"Hello there." From behind the counter, Addison smiled up at him. "You're early."

"Am I?" He glanced at his wristwatch and resisting the urge to slip behind the reception counter and scoop her into his arms for a delicious pre-dinner kiss, he squatted by the small pen and scratched the puppies' ears. "They've grown quite a bit."

"Puppies do that at this age."

"I'm surprised they're still here. They're awfully cute."

"Aren't they though." She came from around the counter and squatted beside him, each scratching behind the ears of a rambunctious little dog with viciously wagging tails.

"There's been a slight change of plan." Kyle kept his focus on the fluffy puppy's ears.

Still scratching and petting the one puppy, Addison lifted the other out of the pen and set him on the floor. "What kind of change?"

Before he could respond, the little puppy suddenly freed from his confinement, with enough energy to power a small city, came rushing at him, knocking him off his feet and flat onto his back. Kyle lifted himself into a sitting position, and without delay, the dog curled into his lap. Tail sweeping the floor, the pup lovingly licked his hand.

"I think he likes you."

"Probably smells the BLT I had for lunch earlier today."

"Or he's got good instincts. Most dogs do."

He couldn't help but grin up at her, but resisted the urge to ask what did her instincts tell her. Instead he explained the change in plans. "My grandmother invited you to dinner tonight. My grandfather insisted I agree. Hope you don't mind?"

"Not at all. I enjoyed the company last time."

"This time there won't be a crowd. Only the four of us. My brother Mitch might join us. He stores an airplane in one of the barns. Has been working on it for years."

"As in building his own plane?"

Kyle nodded.

"You really do have a very interesting family." She smiled sweetly.

Happily, he returned the smile. "Thank you."

Apparently aware that he'd been left alone in the pen, the other puppy began to whimper softly. Addison lifted it out and just like his sibling, the not-so little puppy flew in his direction and once again he found himself flat on his back only this time with a dog at each side, licking his face. Eyes squeezed shut, he muttered, "We really should stop meeting this way."

Despite his efforts to extricate himself from all the energetic puppy love, the two little guys were faster than he was. Something that would not have been the case ten years ago. Another sign that maybe it was time to consider his time on the circuit would be coming to an end sooner than later. Even though his doctor had given him a clean bill of health to return to the racing in a couple of weeks, and his time in the simulators showed his reflexes were as good as ever, the puppies now sitting on his chest and licking his face told a different story as to where his future was heading. Glancing up at Addison staring down and smiling at him and more likely the tail wagging energetic furballs, his heart swelled in his chest. For the first time in his life, he just might have something more important to him than a race.

"I don't know that they're going to let you go. I'm thinking you may have to take them with you."

"I move around too much. Spend most of my off-season time on the *Baroness*, and many of the countries I travel to have very strict regulations on dogs and quarantines."

She shrugged. "You strike me as a man who thinks well outside the box."

That he was. So many things about this moment were

totally outside the box for more than one part of his life. The puppies. His career. This woman. Definitely time to rethink everything he thought was important. And soon, before he lost his chance.

"Better say a prayer." Kyle hopped out of the driver side and hurried around to Addison's passenger door.

"I don't think you'll need them." She'd been delighted to discover that he'd opted to pick her up in one of the ranch pickup trucks. That alone made it easier for her to point out that destiny was on their side.

"You say that now, but my grandparents haven't had dogs in the house for at least a decade. I'm sure if they wanted one, they would have gotten one."

"Maybe they just didn't realize how much they needed a puppy in their life."

On the way to dinner they'd paused at the pet shop and bought all the required accoutrements for the animals. Once Kyle had come to terms with the idea that he wasn't leaving the shelter without one of the puppies that had accosted him so lovingly, he toiled over which one to bring to the ranch. Each one had fallen head over paws in love with Kyle, and from the sparkle in his eyes and occasional burst of laughter at their antics, she knew he'd fallen in love with them too. When he finally admitted he didn't have the heart to leave one behind, her own heart had fallen just a little bit more for him. As if she wasn't already well on her way to tumbling completely head over heels for this guy.

"So, what's the plan?" she asked.

He looked at all the bags in the backseat of the quad cab and then considered the side by side crate. When he spotted the two pups dozing in the separate crates with their backs touching through the caged wires, the corners of his lips tipped upward. "Something tells me we're only going to need one crate."

"Maybe for now." Whenever a family adopted a shelter

pet, the staff was always left with a good feeling. Watching Kyle take these little guys home gave her the warm and fuzzies all over.

Tapping the tailgate with his ring, Kyle took a step back. "Maybe breaking Grams in slowly is the better way to go."

"Not the Governor?"

He shook his head. "Whatever Grams wants, Grams gets. She's the one who we have to convince."

"Okay." She extended her hand. "We're in this together."

"Together." He grinned at her, squeezed her hand, and made her heart beat just a little faster. She really liked that idea.

Sitting in the front parlor, Lila Baron smiled up as they entered the room. "I had thought you'd be here sooner."

"We had to run an errand on the way home." Kyle gestured for Addison to take a seat on the sofa, then without letting go of her hand, sat beside her. "I brought you a little gift."

"Two, actually." Addison smiled sweetly, hoped she hadn't spoken out of turn, and really hoped Kyle's grandparents would get on board. With this much land for the dogs to roam and maybe even chase a few cows, they'd probably live long and extremely happy lives.

"Oh." Lila's smile grew wider. "I love surprises. What do you have?"

Kyle glanced at Addison, lifted one brow, and to her surprise she realized she understood perfectly what he was asking. Should they go get the puppies now, or ease the older couple into the idea. Not sure which was the right answer, Addison merely shrugged one shoulder and flipped her free hand palm up in an unsure gesture. With a nod of understanding, he pushed to his feet, muttering, "Might as well get this over with."

"We'll be right back. I'll get the surprise from the truck. Keep your eyes closed."

Lila Baron closed her eyes and the Governor frowned.

"You too, sir."

The old man's brows shot up in surprise and then with a resigned sigh, he did as he was told.

Out the front door and down the steps, Addison unlatched one crate and snapped her fingers for the puppy who had already woken up. "Funny, I'm not as sure about this as I was a little while ago."

Kyle grabbed the second pup and cradled him in his arms. "Don't chicken out on me now."

"No, sir." She grinned and together they made their way back into the house.

Once inside, Kyle set the first puppy down at the grandmother's feet and gestured with his chin for Addison to do the same with the Governor. Keeping a firm hand on its back so it wouldn't jump up and startle them, Kyle sucked in a deep breath. "You can look now."

At the same time his grandmother's eyes opened wide, Kyle let go of the puppy, who for a fraction of a second almost seemed to turn to Kyle for permission before licking the older woman's shoe and then gently pawing at her leg.

"I think he wants you to pick him up," Kyle said.

"Oh. My." Lila stared for a long minute. Unlike with Kyle, the puppy didn't pounce, it merely sat with his tail wagging, waiting for the older woman to do something.

"Aren't you a polite little fellow?" One side of Lila's mouth tipped upward in the same way Addison had seen Kyle grin when an idea was growing on him.

So intent on how Lila was reacting, it took Addison another moment to realize the Governor already had his puppy in his lap and had stroked it to sleep. How the heck had he done that so fast?

The old man was clearly a mind reader. His gaze met Addison's and all the gruff and rough edges she'd seen last time had melted behind those smiling eyes. "Call me a dog whisperer."

Lila sniffed. "I thought I didn't want my heart broken again."

The Governor reached his hand out and gently patted his wife's knee. Now Addison understood why they'd gone a decade without new dogs.

"I think I may have been wrong." Wiping a single tear from one eye and then lifting the puppy into her lap, she shifted her attention to her grandson. "They're a lovely gift."

Two seconds later the puppy peed in her lap and as Addison's jaw dropped in horror, Lila Baron surprised her with a deep own belly laugh. "Oh, we're going to have to teach you better manners."

From the second Addison had looked at him with those saucer-like eyes and told him the pups were meant for him, he knew she was right. Sort of. They were meant to be in the Baron household where he'd see them at Sunday dinners and other longer visits. The way his grandmother lit up talking to the pups and settling them in to their new home in the laundry room for now with the beds in the parlor and extra beds ordered for their room, he loved Addison even more for convincing him to take a chance on the pups.

And yes, he had no choice but to admit that he had fallen deep and hard for Addison. She was definitely the one person on the planet meant for him. All he had to do was figure out how to convince her of that.

To his surprise, his brother Mitch had joined them for dinner after working on the plane awhile. At first he hadn't given much thought to how much time Mitch spent at the ranch. After all, every Baron grandchild loved the place and loved being blessed with healthy and loving grandparents, but they had lives. Mitch's flights back and forth from Washington seemed to have increased. Kyle might want to talk to Craig and Chase about it. See if they knew what might be going on. Although, the intuitive one in the family was Eve. Maybe he should start with her.

"So I hear you've been medically cleared?" Mitch took a bite of roast beef.

Kyle nodded. "Doc gave me the a-ok and my last few practice sessions getting out of the harness and removing the steering wheel have been consistently under the required five seconds. I'm going to hit the track in Austin for the official approval and if all goes well I'll be taking my spot back in the line up."

"Good thing." Mitch reached for his water. "For a reserve driver in a single race or two Gibs isn't bad, but he just doesn't have your sense of timing to carry a season. Last week he blocked too late and sent three cars spinning out."

"Did the same thing two weeks before that. Even I know you aren't supposed to move when you brake," Lila added.

The Governor nodded. "The team will be happy to have you back."

Kyle nodded. He'd watched the races carefully and the two crashes only two weeks apart had him pushing himself to return as fast as possible. At least for the rest of the season.

"So you'll be racing in Austin next week?" Addison's voice came out less than steady.

"I really think so."

Her lips pressed together, she set her fork down and nodding, reached for her glass of water.

"We should all go." Mitch smiled at Addison. Bless his big brother, trying to put Addison at ease making his risky job a family affair.

"Yes." Lila nodded.

That had Kyle whipping his head around. His grandmother had been to one race live and never gone back again. As far as he knew, she didn't even like to watch the races on television.

"Then it's a plan." The Governor finalized the choice for everyone.

Addison's eyes flickered from one family member to the other before leveling with Kyle's.

"I'd love to have you there," he said softly, daring to reach for her free hand.

Very slowly she nodded. "I'm sure it will be lovely."

She didn't sound terribly convinced, but he had to make

her see that as dangerous as racing was, all the advances through recent years had made his job very safe. Because he was sure of one thing already, if he had to choose between the career he loved and the woman he loved, the answer was a no brainer.

CHAPTER FIFTEEN

Apparently, a day at the races actually meant a weekend at the races. Another thing Addison had learned about the rich and famous was not only did they all have an awful lot of expensive cars, they owned a lot of nice homes too. In this case, the Baron family kept a weekend cottage for the one weekend a year that Kyle raced in Austin and for the week of the South by Southwest Festival. The confusion seemed to be with vocabulary. For Addison, a cottage didn't bring to mind a five thousand square foot home with seven bedrooms and a killer view of the hill country.

Eve had noticed right away that she had felt a tad overwhelmed upon their arrival. "I don't know about you, but I love girls' nights."

"Girls' nights?" Addison repeated.

"Yep." Eve looped her elbow with Addison and slowly walked her deeper into the large home. "You and I are sharing a room. I brought a stash of cheddar popcorn, chips, Kerbey's famed queso, and my favorite white merlot."

She already knew she liked Eve, but at that moment Addison was eternally grateful to the lady for making her laugh, and for bringing the wine. Now bright and early the next morning, the merlot might not have been her best idea. The two of them had a great time giggling and laughing until almost three in the morning. Her favorite had been the stories of Kyle as a little kid.

Now she sat between Eve and Craig Baron, staring down from their comfy and air conditioned seats at a much larger and different looking track than where Kyle had taken her for a ride.

"How much do you know about how this works?" Craig leaned into her.

"Kyle explained it to me." Not that she'd followed all of it, but she'd almost had a heart attack when she realized how much money was involved in racing. Somewhere in passing she discovered that the top tier made millions. And not just one or two but double digit millions.

"So you know that Baron Industries sponsors Kyle's team."

She nodded. She was also flummoxed to learn that the team consisted of hundreds of people, from mechanics to engineers to managers to public relations. The list was long. Oddly enough, the most interesting tidbit for the day was learning that the steering wheel was rectangular not round, and that the cars weren't controlled by foot pedals but from the steering wheel. The thing that kept throwing her off early on was the difference between the pit and the pit wall. Now that she sat in the family's luxury box, she had a birds-eye view of everything, and slowly, everything that had been shared with her began to make sense.

"This is where we're going to see for real if Kyle is still in good form." Eve turned to face her. "If he makes it to the top ten for starting position that will be decent. Top five will be better."

"But not ideal," she put out.

Eve shook her head. "For the bottom five eliminated in the first wave, and the second five eliminated after that, top ten would be glorious. Not so much for Kyle."

"He is a bit competitive."

"A bit?" Eve teased, but the two women burst into a fit of giggles.

Addison's nerves were already beginning to settle just a tiny bit. The first qualifiers started and scanning the distance in search of Kyle's car, she scooted to the edge of her seat. Cars zoomed around, speeding by. So far so good. No crashes, no mishaps, and boy did those pit crews change tires fast!

"Okay, so now we're down to the top fifteen cars vying for the top ten starting positions." Eve pointed out Kyle's

Team Baron car, and Addison swallowed hard, telling herself not to grip the arms of the chair so tightly or someone might notice she was getting nervous again. To her surprise, keeping her gaze focused on Kyle's car actually helped her keep calm. He was going so fast that before she knew what happened, he'd managed to ease forward a spot or two and she was actually out of her seat and clapping madly. The enthusiasm in the luxury box was at high levels when a car just a little behind Kyle clipped another car sending them both careening into the wall.

Bits of car flew through the air. Tires came off and rolled down the track. Addison's hands flew to her mouth and she took a step forward. A red flag appeared but not before another car spun around the debris and tumbled over. Suddenly there was a smoking pile of multiple cars. The bigger surprise for her was when all the drivers appeared from their broken and mangled cars and literally walked it off.

"They've come a long way with safety." Lila Baron placed a warm hand on Addison's forearm. "Even just a few years ago they added the halo bar to save even more lives. As dangerous as it could be, he'll be fine."

All Addison could do was nod. Not till the track had been cleared, the final wave placing Kyle third in the starting lineup completed, and following Craig and Eve downstairs and out of the building and over to the Team Baron area where she was able to see Kyle did she breathe easy again. She couldn't even begin to imagine how she'd feel had he been one of the cars in the pile up. Or worse.

"So, what's your take on this?" Sitting sideways in the large rocker, her foot dangling over the arm, Eve took a sip of her wine.

Forearms resting on the railing, Craig looked over his shoulder at his little sister. "This what?"

"The weather," she huffed sarcastically. "Kyle and

Addison. What else?"

"She's nice." Craig returned to gazing off into the distance. At night, with the city lit up below, the view from the house was as dazzling as the daytime view was breathtaking.

"I know that. There have been a lot of nice girls come and go through the doors of this family. I'm thinking more that I've never seen Kyle quite so….not sure what the word is."

"In love," Mitch offered quickly from his seat across from his sister. "Speaking of which, where are the lovebirds?"

Craig lifted his chin toward the hill below. "Taking a walk. Addison still seemed a bit on edge at dinner. I suspect he's trying to convince her that his life isn't in danger every time he gets behind the wheel of a race car."

"Wait a minute. Back up." Eve shifted, dropping her feet to the floor and leaning forward, her brother Mitch in her sights. "What do you mean in love?"

"You know. L. O. V. E. That thing that adults do just before they marry and repopulate the earth." A heavy curtain of sadness drew down over Mitch's eyes. Whether it was for the loss of his beloved late wife, or mourning the children they'd never found the time to have, Eve wasn't sure. But her brother was indeed confirming her own suspicions. Suspicions she hadn't dared voice out loud.

"I agree." Craig turned around to face his siblings. "The question I have is whether she's going to leave him when all this gets to be too much or if he's going to leave racing before she gets worn down by the stress."

Now both her brothers had her attention. "Do you really think he'd stop racing?"

"You do know that he was discussing retiring at dinner the other night?" Mitch raised a brow at his sister. "Has *that* ever happened before?"

Eve shook her head. A lot of things had never happened before. Starting with Addison making it through more than one family dinner. Most of the women her brothers dated, except for CJ and Abbie, came and went quickly. And if

Chase and Mitch were any indication, when they fall in love, her brothers fall hard and fast.

On their way back to the house, Eve could hear Kyle reassuring Addison. "You saw for yourself that even with a pile up, the cars are designed to be very safe."

Eve had no idea if Addison was speaking softly, or if she had merely moved her head in assent or disagreement.

"Do you trust me?" Eve heard Kyle say from where they stood at the foot of the deck.

This time she heard Addison respond ever so softly, "More than I thought possible."

The silence between them lingered and it took Eve a few more moments before curiosity got the better of her and pushing to her feet, she leaned over the side of the railing to see the couple in the shadows below. Expecting to find a passionate locking of lips, instead she looked just long enough to see Addison curled against Kyle, her head resting on his shoulder and Kyle leaning in to give her a comforting peck on the temple.

Dear Heaven. Mitch was right. Kyle was most definitely head over heels in love with Addison.

The patio door slid open and to her surprise, only Kyle appeared. "Addison is worn out. She's gone ahead to bed."

"I'll just finish this up, then I'll go join her." Eve held her glass up for her brother to see it was nearly empty.

"Thanks." Kyle smiled. "I'd appreciate that. I suspect she could use some alone time to process the day and decompress, but I don't want her alone too long."

"No worries." Eve could get used to this role of sister-in-law, and friend. She loved CJ to death, but Chase and his wife lived in Dallas so she didn't have much opportunity to spend time with the recent addition of a wife and sister to the family tree. Even though Kyle traveled the world with the racing circuit, on the downtime, she'd get to see him, and now maybe Addison. Of course, she was probably putting the cart before the horse. Who knew if this whole thing would blow up any minute, but if she were a betting woman, her money would be on golden wedding anniversary plans.

CHAPTER SIXTEEN

Being fully suited up yesterday for the qualifying races had felt pretty darn good to Kyle. Coming in third for the lineup hadn't been bad either. Considering how many weeks he'd been away from behind the wheel, and how many weeks it had been before he could fully rehab his wrist, he was perfectly content with third place in the starting lineup. Now standing waiting to get into his vehicle, he felt the full adrenaline rush that made him love this job. How could he walk away while he still had the right stuff? The question brought a beautiful face to mind.

"Looking good, man." Gibs, the reserve driver who had taken his spot on the team during his convalescence slapped him on the back. "You've been missed."

Kyle nodded. "Thanks. Good to be back." His gaze lifted to the grandstand and the private luxury suite he knew his family would be watching from. At this distance he could barely make out the approximate area where the suite was, never mind figure out who the small dots inside were. He wondered what Addison was doing up there. There was no doubt she was getting along well with his family. She and Eve already got along like a house on fire and he was pretty sure given time they would be cohorts in all sorts of shenanigans. What he really wished was that he could have seen Addison before leaving for the race. Heck, he wouldn't mind having her here at his side for a good luck kiss.

Tiny pricks of excitement mingled with a hint of anxiousness. For him, the anxiousness was something new. He didn't need that interfering with his focus, his goal, and yet, he had to wonder if this was merely Mother Nature's way of protecting the species. Find love, marry, hang up your driving gloves, make babies. Shaking his head, he cleared his thoughts. Bachelors didn't have an edge over married men in this biz. He needed to focus. Like it or not, he needed to push thoughts of Addison aside and keep his mind on nothing but the track and the race.

"Ready?" one of his crew chiefs called over to him.

Kyle nodded. "Ready."

Adrenaline skyrocketing again, he secured his gear and climbed into the driver's seat. A grin tugged at the corners of his mouth. Life was more than good.

Kyle had left the house before Addison and Eve had made their way downstairs. The difference between this house and the main family ranch, and what apparently made it a cottage in the family's eyes, was that there were no servants. The family did the cooking and cleaning up after themselves. Addison hadn't given it much thought, but until this little visit she would have suspected no one in the family would know how to boil water, never mind prepare an entire meal. They actually, once again, proved to be like everyone else she knew. As it turned out, Eve and Mitch were actually darn good cooks. She almost swallowed her tongue watching the Senator chop vegetables like one of those television chefs. As odd as it sounded, it made her feel better about voting for him. A well-rounded guy who she suspected was proficient in many matters.

"What would you like to drink?" a deep voice asked from over her shoulder.

Addison turned in her seat to notice a waiter patiently waiting. "Diet cola, please. No ice."

The young man nodded and turned away, asking the same question of Mrs. Baron.

On the track, the cars were moving in what to her nervous system seemed like slow motion. Rounding the wide space, one by one the cars lined up at the starting line in two rows of ten cars each. "I see why making the top spot in the line up is important. Has to be tough for the guys in the back."

"Definitely not easy, but occasionally you see someone come out on top," Mrs. Baron explained sweetly.

"Especially if it's a better driver who simply had a mishap during qualifiers," Mitch added.

"Watch the lights." Eve pointed. "One red light. Two, Three."

Another second and as the lights dimmed, the announcer called out the obvious, "lights out" and the cars took off in earnest.

Addison's heart skipped a beat, her gaze locked on the bright yellow car representing Team Baron. Within moments, Kyle shifted right and almost made his way around the car in front of him. From this distance it looked as if he'd almost clipped the other guy's rear bumper. Silently she reminded herself that everything looked closer from a distance. Then she added the mantra that Kyle was one of the best. The man knew what he was doing, and she had little doubt he was going to try again, and soon.

Another few moments and his car was no longer visible through the suite's large window. Anyone interested in the remaining portions of the track had to shift their attention to the wall of screens to the side. From there they could track different portions of the race. The remote controls at Mitch's fingertips, he zoomed in on the view from Kyle's dash cam. The movement had Addison squeezing her seat arms more tightly.

Yesterday she'd learned more about his support team. The pit crew alone had over twenty people to change out the tires in under three seconds. That boggled her mind. It took her longer than that to find the jack. Not only were there a plethora of nutritionists and trainers and managers and PR people, there were also the expected strategists, engineers, and mechanics both here and at the factory behind the scenes on computers and simulators. The key players were in constant communication with Kyle, sharing strategies, track conditions, pit stop needs, and miscellaneous details about the other drivers and their positions. The bigger surprise for her wasn't just that modern technology had all these people communicating live and in the moment—after all, as an engineer the concept wasn't foreign to her—the unexpected had been that both the family and the fans were privy to the conversations.

On several screens on the opposite wall were the television broadcasts of the race. The announcers made their commentaries on many of the drivers' actions as well as the team communications. Along with the television commentators, the Barons kept their team's radio communications on loud and clear. After the first hour of watching the cars go round and round, in and out of the pit, slow down for a red flag when a driver lost a tire, or in the case of Kyle's teammate had a wheel freeze up and the car had to crawl its way to the pit, she'd failed to understand the overall appeal of the race.

On the other hand, she also better understood that despite the insane speeds at which all the cars were traveling, the scenario was indeed not as dangerous as she had originally thought. Not that it was a walk in the park, but it was clear that the system was not reckless, and that even when things went wrong, every precaution had been taken before a mishap to keep the drivers safe.

As much as she'd been glued to her seat, the family had gotten up and moved around. For a bit, the Governor and Mitch had sat side by side talking political shop. The two apparently disagreed strongly about the outcome of some special state committee. Eve and Craig had gotten into a heated discussion over driving skills versus driver hot factor, Craig insisting that dreamy eyes and a sexy nickname was not a key factor in driver fame. Eve held a different opinion, and a fondness for a German fellow with a rather juvenile nickname Addison had already forgotten.

Mrs. Baron on the other hand had stuck close to Addison's side and either coincidentally or quite intentionally distracted her with chit chat at some of Kyle's most hairpin turns or passes. The sweet woman patted Addison's arm. "I think it's time to stretch our legs and have a little snack." She didn't wait for her to respond, the woman merely stood and turned toward the spread of food across the room, fully expecting Addison to follow. Which of course she did.

She certainly had to give the woman credit for timing. Not only did the food spread across two tables look absolutely delicious, her stomach growled in agreement.

"You have to try the crab cake crostinis." Eve held one out for her to take. "They are absolutely to die for."

"If you're fond of seafood," Mitch pointed to the opposite end of the table, "the calamari marinara is delicious and hard to come by in our state."

"True." Eve sighed. "Why so many restaurants are enamored with frying I'll never know."

Addison didn't have an answer for her newfound friend. As a matter of fact, until this very moment, her Texas-born self had no idea there was any other way to eat calamari. Her plate filled with all the different suggestions, she returned to her seat. Nibbling on the morsels between glancing up at the screens when Kyle was around the track and back as he came around in front of the grandstand, she decided Eve and Mitch were absolutely right. Calamari marinara was the bomb.

"Last lap coming up." The Governor leaned forward in his seat. "This is Kyle's last chance to take the lead."

"Do you think he can do it?" she dared to ask.

A few heads nodded yes, and a few others shrugged. It was Mrs. Baron who softly responded, "Anything is possible."

The calamari and shrimp forgotten, Addison's gaze remained glued to the big screen. Even with her lack of understanding, it was pretty obvious Kyle was doing his best to find his way around the driver in the number one spot. From the conversation, not all terribly polite, between Kyle and his engineers, it was pretty clear they did not agree on the best way to accomplish the move.

As he made his way out of the first half of the lap and the car in third inched closer to Kyle, she found herself literally sitting on the edge of her seat. Just a little while longer, and the day would be behind her. How did racing wives handle the stress? Hearing her own thoughts, she sat up straight. How in the world could she compare herself to a racer's wife? She wasn't even sure if what they had could be called dating. The car on Kyle's heels pulled in tighter and her heart clenched. She had her answer. Because she was totally and completely in love with Kyle Baron.

"Shit," came across loud and clear on the radio, snapping her out of her own thoughts.

Apparently she wasn't the only one to notice that the top three cars were too close for a lot of people's comfort. A person didn't have to be an engineer to understand that driving at that high a speed and tailgating didn't bode well. As the three cars took the last turn, the first one pulled just enough ahead to give Addison a smidge of breathing room, when the third car made his move and on cue from the strategist on the radio, or maybe it was an engineer, someone cued Kyle and he moved to block.

Back on the edge of her seats, she gripped the chair arm again. "Step on it!" she shouted to Kyle.

Mitch chuckled. "Sounds like she's getting the hang of this."

"Shh." His grandmother waved him off, clearly as gripped by the last minute moves as Addison was.

The next thing Addison knew, the older lady had stretched her hand out and clutched tightly onto Addison's hand at the same moment the third car made a last ditch move, and clipped the back end of Kyle's car.

Someone screeched, a chorus of gasps punctuated by a few "Oh Gods" filled the room. The tire flew off the racecar, sending Kyle into a spin. The other car flipped right over him, sending the two cars into somersaults. Mrs. Baron's grip on her right hand tightened and her left hand flew to her mouth. "It's okay," she said to herself over and over. With every effort to calm herself down, the car worked against her. Flipping over and over, the sliding and skipping and finally crashing into the side wall, the other car landing almost on top of it.

The only thing she could think was to pray Dear Lord

don't let it catch on fire. She'd seen a video of a race car engulfed in flames once. Watching a total stranger, even knowing he'd survived, was still enough to send her already jittery nerves into overload.

"Please be okay," she whispered softly.

Mrs. Baron whispered back, "Amen."

The chatter on the radio was loud and overwhelming. She could hear their team calling to him. "Are you okay? Kyle, are you all right?" The silence on the other end was only made more frightening by the sight of men running, some with fire extinguishers, others with who knew what to extricate a potentially severely injured man. Her heart alternated between racing too fast and nearly stopping.

Immediately her mind flew back to Kyle's comments about needing to be able to undo the harness and remove the steering wheel in less than five seconds. Both necessary to get out of the car. It had been way more than five seconds and he still wasn't out.

Everyone's eyes remained glued to the scene on the other side of the glass. If she was seeing correctly, the rescue team had removed Kyle from the remnants of the car, seat and all. Ambulances arrived, blocking what little there was of her view.

"He'll be taken to the medical tent," the Governor said aloud, though she got the feeling he was talking to himself more than the rest of them.

Mitch had a phone in hand and was quietly, yet forcefully, demanding answers from whoever was on the other end of the line.

Unable to make out what was happening, now that the ambulance had pulled away, she and the others turned to Mitch.

Blowing out a deep breath, he blinked hard, holding his eyes closed for a few seconds longer than necessary. "They're taking him straight to the hospital."

CHAPTER SEVENTEEN

Never had Addison been so caught up in a whirlwind of activity. The entire family had piled into their cars. Except rather than drive to the hospital, they traveled a short distance to the nearest heliport. Flying to the hospital was not the way that Addison would have liked to have experienced her first helicopter ride. She was, however, thankful for anything that got her to Kyle's side sooner than later.

Eve had been the first Baron to arrive at the hospital, but had been unable to retrieve any information on Kyle's condition. Addison flew in the same chopper as the Governor and Mrs. Baron. Much to her surprise, from the moment they'd stepped out of the helicopter on the hospital's rooftop, Lila Baron had grabbed hold of the crook of Addison's arm and not let go. Together they rode down the elevator and followed the Governor and Senator marching to the reception desk.

Only moments after Mitch flashed his Senate ID, and the Governor loudly announced the familial relationship with Kyle Baron, the nurse clacked away at her keyboard and with little information to share dared to take on the two politicians. "I've notified the nurses' station that you are here. As soon as there is any word, somebody will come and get you." Clacking his cane on the floor, the Governor opened his mouth to speak, but the nurse cut him off with an openhanded palm. "I'm sorry, but until a physician gives the okay, you'll only be in the way. I assume you want what's best for your family member?" The comment was neither subtle nor veiled. The lady would make a good politician herself.

Gritting his back teeth, the Governor nodded and spun around with such agility that for a short moment Addison wondered if he needed the cane at all.

Together she and Lila, arms still linked, made their way to the sparsely decorated waiting room. Her stomach churning and tears threatening to spill, she needed something to do beside worry if the man she loved was alive or dead or something unpleasantly in between.

Waiting for the older woman to sit, Addison looked briefly around for anything that resembled a vending machine or signs for a cafeteria. "I think I'll go see if I can find some coffee. Would you like one?"

Lila shook her head. "No, dear. Thank you."

Quickly she asked the others now seated in the corner of the waiting room if they'd like anything from the cafeteria. As each person shook their head, she debated leaving for the sake of having something to do or staying with this family she'd grown so close to in only a short while. Needing to do something, anything, even if it meant buying a cup of coffee she didn't really want to drink was better than quietly wringing her hands in desperation. "I'll be right back."

"Want me to go with you?" Eve offered.

The gesture was almost enough to make Addison smile. Almost, but not quite. "No, thanks. I won't be long."

Backtracking to the reception desk, she kept a close eye on the ER doors. Hoping deep down that at any second a doctor would come out to tell the family that all was well, or better yet, Kyle would stroll out himself, flashing his toe curling smile at her.

By the time she reached the desk she'd taken note of something else. Once the receptionist buzzed a person in, or if hospital personnel keyed themselves in, the doors stayed open for a long few minutes.

"May I help you?" the same nurse asked.

She dragged her gaze away from the door. "Where can I get a coffee?"

"There's a vending machine down the hall toward the front lobby, but you'll get a better cup if you go to the cafeteria on the second floor." The woman turned and stretching her arm straight out, pointed to a pair of elevators just past the doors to the ER's inner sanctum.

"Thanks." She did her best to offer a sincere smile. Especially now that she had a plan.

For the third time in the last several minutes, a doctor flashed a light into Kyle's eyes. "I'm sure nothing has changed since the last two times someone's done that. I'm fine. If you would please sign me out." Kyle pushed to sit up, and overcome by a wave of nausea, leaned back down again.

"And that is why we're not signing you out." The doctor waved a finger at him.

"Well, I'm not staying here. And where is my family?"

Listening to Kyle's chest, the man stared at some unknown point. "If you mean Governor Baron, he is not very quietly in the waiting room with a few others."

"Great." Kyle blew out a sigh and flung his arm over his eyes. The overhead light was giving him a killer headache. "Has anyone told them I'm all right?"

"Hospital policy is not to report to family until we are sure of what we're reporting."

"You may not be sure, but I am. I'm fine and I want to go home. Trust me when I tell you my grandmother will take better care of me than you can."

This time the man smiled. "I'm sure she'd do a great job, but that doesn't change the fact that you've had one hell of a blow to the head. You were knocked unconscious and did not come to until after the ambulance was on its way. Like it or not, you're staying for observation overnight."

"We'll see about that." The words were no sooner out of his mouth than the doorway from the ER must have opened because suddenly he could hear his grandfather's roar loud and clear. Frankly, Kyle was a bit surprised that the old man hadn't called in the National Guard or a Marine battalion to break into the ER. Suddenly it struck him that he hoped no one had called his mother. Having her fly halfway around the world to discover he was perfectly fine was not in anyone's best interest.

The curtain that separated him from the rest of the ER slid open and a petite nurse smiled at him, then turned to the doctor. "The Governor and Senator have been on the phone with the Chief of Staff. Shall I go get them before they call in the National Guard?"

Kyle almost laughed. Apparently the gal was a pretty good judge of character, but it was the sight behind the astute nurse that caught his eye and had him almost leaping out of bed. That was if movement didn't keep making him dizzy.

At that second, Addison turned and saw him. Immediately, she pivoted and shifted direction, almost flying into the small curtained cubicle. "You're all right." Practically bulldozing over the doctor, performing the perfect hip check to nudge him out of her way, she ran her fingers along Kyle's cheek, her gaze following the IV tubing. "You *are* all right, aren't you?"

"We're waiting on the results of the x-rays and MRI, but so far he appears to have a mild concussion."

"The sooner someone gets my grandfather in here, the sooner I'll be on my way home."

Her hand in his, she pulled back. "I'll go get him. Your grandmother will want to see for herself that you're okay."

"No." He squeezed her hand more tightly and pulled her closer to him. "Please stay. Someone else can go get them."

A hint of a smile teased at the corners of her mouth, but he couldn't read the expression in her eyes. He thought perhaps he saw pain or worry, or some combination of both and hated that he'd caused it.

With the curtains drawn, they could see a different set of doors fly open and a couple of paramedics rushing a gurney into the building and follow a nurse's direction to another cubicle.

The doctor's gaze lifted to the commotion and one foot already moving away, he turned to Kyle. "You stay put. I mean it." Hurrying away, it surprised Kyle that the man took the extra second to drag the curtain almost closed. Kyle would need to remember to thank him for the little bit of extra privacy. As sure as he knew his name was Kyle Baron, he knew any second now he'd be barraged by worried Barons.

"I'm sorry," he said.

"For what?"

"Making you worry."

Addison tried to smile. "I'm just glad you're okay. Or, mostly okay."

"I'm going to be just fine as soon as the room stops spinning."

Her eyes narrowed with concern as she shifted away from the bed.

"No." He tugged her close and patted the bedside for her to sit down again. "It feels better with you here. Close." He closed his eyes briefly and sucked in a fortifying breath, then blew it out slowly. He wasn't risk adverse, so as far as he was concerned, there was no time like the present to jump in feet first. "You've made everything better since the day I met you."

Tension eased from her shoulders and a smile pulled at her cheeks. "Back at you."

"I'm not being polite, I'm serious."

She bobbed her head and smiled. "So was I."

"Good. Then you won't be at all surprised when I tell you that I have been chasing the adrenaline high my whole life."

Her smile slipped, she shook her head, and squeezed his hand.

"Well, I've finally figured a few things out." He sucked in a slow deep breath. Here went nothing. "I don't need to run with the bulls, jump out of planes, or drive at two hundred miles an hour to be high on life. All I need is you. I love you."

Her eyes opened wide and round and then to his relief, her smile returned. "I'm glad, because it turns out I love you too. Very much."

"I can quit racing."

"But you love it."

"I love you more. If going through another incident like this again is too much, I can stop. It doesn't matter anymore." And to his surprise, he meant every syllable. No matter how much he loved racing. No matter how little the accidents and mishaps bothered him. No matter how big his chances of taking it all this year, nothing mattered more than keeping Addison in his life—forever.

"While I can't think of words to tell you how much that means to me, that you'd give up your dreams for me—"

"I—"

With a finger on his lips, she cut him off. "I would never ask you to give up your dreams. I'll find a way to live with it. And you."

"We'll find a way. From now on my life is about us."

Her grin widened from ear to ear and there was no way he could resist kissing it off her pretty face. Whether it was the power of her kiss, or the power of the concussion that left him light headed, he wasn't sure, but he was positive that the sound of multiple clearing throats is what had them pulling away from each other. Addison lifted off the bed and took a step away when he grabbed her hand and pulled her close to the bedside again.

"The doctor tells us you're spending the night." The Governor looked from him to her and back. "Anything else we should know?"

The only one with a serious expression was the Governor. The rest of his family all stood back like a bunch of cats smiling with canary feathers in their teeth.

"As someone who has watched you race through life and drag your feet on matters of the heart, I'm delighted you finally see the wisdom in embracing the important things in life." His grandmother stepped forward, shook her head at him, leaned in to kiss his cheek and whispered in his ear, "What took you so long?"

EPILOGUE

"I don't know how she does it." CJ Baron stood beside Eve. "My blood pressure is having a hard enough time watching my brother-in-law speed around the track faster than a category five hurricane. I can't imagine how I'd feel if the man I loved were the one behind the wheel."

Didn't Eve know exactly what her sister-in-law meant? Growing up watching her brother speed in anything with four wheels, regardless of risk, left her less than disinterested in dating, never mind marrying, an adrenaline junkie. But danged if every time she turned around, Kyle and Addison looked like a pair of precious bookends. Suitable for a collection of romantic bric-a-brac.

Eve was beginning to get used to seeing not one but two of her brothers fall head over boot heel in love, but a tinge of something very similar to the green-eyed monster prickled at the back of her neck. The part of her that grew up believing in fairytales and Prince Charming wondered if she'd ever get that lucky in love. Then there was the practical side who had spent the better part of a decade studying to be the best of the best, and then, battling the good old boys to sit at the head of her own very profitable perfume chemical company. That side didn't have time for love. Heck, that side of her didn't really have time for much more than an occasional meal and forty winks. And it certainly wouldn't understand how Addison had turned her nose at an interview for a very lucrative position in Southern California in order to focus on working close to Houston and Kyle's home base. Not that the position she eventually took with one of the largest energy companies in the country wasn't lucrative, but at the time of the other interview, Eve had been sure love was not only blind, it might qualify as pretty dumb, too.

The viewing booth erupted with cheers as Kyle drove the last lap, overtaking the lead, and dragging her back to the moment's reality. Half the family bounced on their feet, screaming as if Kyle had won a presidential election and not a championship race. The other half of the clan hugged and grinned as if they themselves had driven and won the race. The effervescent enthusiasm spread through the room like a storm fueled power surge. A few hugs and cheers and smiling till her face hurt and Eve couldn't have been any happier if she had indeed been in the driver's seat.

Below in the crew area, Addison waited with the Governor and their grandmother. From where she stood, Eve saw the Governor kiss his wife, then turn to hug his future granddaughter-in-law. Fireworks burst overhead, music blared from speakers, and Kyle now stood on the car.

The revelry below was palpable. The entire stadium could feel the energy buzzing through the crew and the crowd. Champagne bottles were passed around and guzzled or poured over heads. It took her another minute of taking it all in to realize Kyle wasn't on the car reveling in his win, he was scanning the growing crowd, looking for someone, and she was pretty sure who that someone was.

Another second or two and Kyle hopped off the hood and took off at a fast gallop. There was only one reason Eve could think of for why her brother would abandon the celebrating and run off away from the crowd. The one reason ran up to him from her spot in the crew's station.

Eve had to admit, even a few short months ago she couldn't imagine her brother abandoning his crew in their most joyous moment. And yet, here she sat like a voyeur watching the two lovebirds make their own music. Only the bottle of champagne a teammate had the audacity—or was it stupidity—to pour over the kissing couple's heads succeeded in garnering their attention.

"Oh, I would so kill someone for doing that." CJ inched forward in her seat, grinning from proverbial ear to ear.

"But look at those two."

Drenched in champagne or not, the two leaned in for one more kiss and circling his arm protectively around her shoulder, Kyle moved them through the crowd to the winners circle. Another slow kiss at the foot of the grandstand and Eve could feel their reluctance to separate clear across the tracks. At this rate she wondered if the two would simply self-combust long before the wedding escape planned in a few weeks.

"They do look happy." Mitch had abandoned his spot by his brothers to come sit by Eve.

"They really do." Eve looked over her shoulder to where CJ had gone to stand by Chase. "They all do."

A soft smile did little to hide the hurt in Mitch's eyes. It made Eve wonder if the old adage *it's better to have loved and lost than never to have loved at all* held any merit. From where she stood, the years of seeing the lingering pain in Mitch's eyes sure didn't seem to be worth it. And yet, the sparkle in Chase and Kyle's gazes sure made Eve want – but what?

Holding the cup high over his head, Kyle grinned for the cameras then quickly handed the cup over to his teammate and leapt over the railing in front of his fiancée. Once again, the two fell into a swoon-worthy clench. Eve's gaze shifted to Chase and CJ, then to Mitch, and back to Kyle and Addison.

Who was she kidding? She wanted what her brothers had found. On a deep sigh, she leaned back in the comfy seat and watched as Kyle and Addison walked hand in hand away from the winners circle. Yep. Whatever her brothers had found, she wanted it too.

Enjoy an excerpt from
Just One Dance

"What you need is a man."

Standing over her latest compound mixture, the dropper in her hand fell to the floor as Eve Baron snapped her head around to face her assistant. "Excuse me?"

"You work too hard." Isabel Santorini had been the best compounder, assistant that Eve had ever worked with. The standard white lab coat did little to hide the woman's gothic wardrobe, complete with heavy combat boots that thudded their way across the commercial linoleum floors. Nor did the plethora of strategically pierced studs along with raven black dyed hair and striking makeup choices give any hint of the brilliant mind that had worked beside Eve since the day she started Le Perfumerie. "I can sense your tension the minute I cross the threshold. You need a good roll in the hay."

"What I need," Eve spun around and handed Isabel a list of her latest choices, "is for you to compound these and leave my love life alone."

"Would love to. If you had one." Isabel flashed a toothy grin. "Love life, that is."

"My love life is just fine. Thank you."

Isabel set a dish of cheese and fresh finger fruits in front of her. "Sure it is. That's why you've been sleeping on the sofa in your office all week."

Eve could do little more than roll her eyes. The woman was right. Eve loved her work, loved being her own boss. From the moment she'd discovered the art of mixing perfumes and that she was darn good at it, better than creating adhesive compounds for safety stickers, she'd strived to build her reputation and her own business. Now it wasn't uncommon that when she worked on a particularly enchanting scent, time would get away from her and she'd crash on the sofa. On the bright side, working crazy long days for stretches at a time kept her from remembering basic necessities like food, which helped keep her in the same size clothes she'd worn since high school. A caring nagger, Isabel made sure that Eve at least didn't starve to death.

"Thanks. I didn't realize I was hungry." Eve popped a morsel of cheese in her mouth.

"For food or men?"

"Will you stop that!" The last thing Eve needed now was a romantic liaison.

"I'm serious. Never mind the roll in the hay. When was the last time you went out on a date?"

"Two weeks ago, at the Shelters for Women annual gala."

One pitch black eyebrow lifted high on Isabel's forehead and her charcoal lips pursed in bitter disagreement. "Jack Preston doesn't count. Even though the man is sexy as hell, he might as well be your brother. Heaven knows no honorable man would be willing to cross the line with his best friend's little sister. Especially when the brother is a Baron and has two more brothers to back him up in a brawl."

There wasn't much of an argument she could give. Jack Preston, her brother Kyle's college buddy, had been her go-to date for charity events and weddings for some time now. It made for great photographs, fed the gossip mill to keep her preferred charities in the news, and repelled unwanted gold-digging male attention. Too bad he wasn't available for tonight's Housing for Heroes event. The entire evening was planned around her joint donation with a major cosmetics company of the naming rights to a recent scent creation. Everyone expected the fundraiser to be a bumper crop night for the non-profit that had done so much for struggling veterans. At least for tonight her grandparents would be in attendance. Not the same as an escort on her arm, but a safe haven nonetheless. Speaking of which, she glanced down at her wrist watch. Three o'clock. If she high-tailed it out of here she'd be able to beat some of the miserable Houston traffic. One of these days she'd move the operation out of downtown, sell her townhouse in the Heights, and set up in a cheaper, less congested northern suburb. Some day.

She tossed a grape in her mouth and a morsel of mozzarella, then scooped the dish into her hand to finish nibbling on her way out the door. "Thanks for the snack, but I need to get moving if I want to wear something other than my lab coat to tonight's banquet."

Isabel stepped back and nodded. Eve was almost out the door when her assistant shouted after her, "If you find a hot bachelor, take him home with you!"

Pepper limping home was the crown on a miserably hot and unproductive day. If today's mishaps were an indication of how tonight would go, Jared Gold was in serious trouble.

"Uh oh." Older than dirt, with legs as bowed as the St Louis arch, there was no man on this planet that Jared would trust with his horses as much as he trusted Randy. "What happened?"

"Good question. We'd barely ridden the first small section of fence on the east pasture when she started favoring one side. I climbed off and checked her shoes, but didn't see anything. I'm guessing she's got a stone bruise. Before we went out this morning I cleaned out some pebbles from her shoes, but you know how it goes."

Salt and pepper brows buckled under loose locks of cayenne red hair. "You wear your boots out walking her all the way back?"

"Just about." Jared patted the horse's neck and scratched under her jaw. "Didn't want to take any chances."

"Smart man." Randy smiled and reached for the reins.

"I'll take a look at her. You'd better be gettin'. Your mama has called me three times in the last hour, looking for you."

"Blast." Jared snapped his fingers and glanced at his phone. Almost five thirty and two missed calls from his mother. "Tonight's that stupid gala. Promised Mom I'd step in for Dad."

"So she said, but isn't this the fundraiser for building homes for troubled or disabled vets?"

Jared nodded.

"Doesn't sound stupid to me."

"No." Jared blew out a long sigh. He stood corrected. The ranch foreman had been like a second father to him for as long as he could remember. Jason Gold was a great dad but had no interest in the ranch that had been in his family since Texas was its own republic. Everything Jared knew about horses and ranching he'd learned first from his Pawpaw, and then from Randy. Everything he'd learned about being a man and a decent human being had come from both his biological and ranch families. "It's a great cause. One I'd be happy to cut a nice check for. It's the dinner and endless superficial chatter that's going to be a stupid way to spend my night."

"Understood." Randy was a cowboy through and through. He'd never survive a night buttoned up in a tuxedo and sipping champagne. Though the way Jared felt at the moment, he wasn't all that sure he'd survive a night dressed like a penguin, making nice to Houston's social elite either.

Handing his horse over, Jared spun around in the direction of the main house. The day he had graduated from A&M, his dad handed him the keys to the front door, all the books for the ranch, including his name on all the banking accounts, and moved himself and his wife into a lush little four thousand square foot house nestled in the heart of a two acre treed lot in the burbs. Both his mom and dad had never been happier.

His next thought was how hard would it be to talk his mother into finding a last minute replacement. Even she would understand any human being would be dead to the world after walking for hours across the ranch on foot with a lame horse. Expecting him to dress up and be social was asking a lot under the circumstances.

"About time." The front door barely latched behind him, his mother appeared in the library doorway. "You're not answering your phone." She sniffed the air. "And you need a shower. A long shower." Despite her announcement of his less than pleasant odiferous contribution to the room, she marched straight up to him and kissed him on his cheek. "We don't want to be late."

All dolled up in a sleek black evening gown, her favorite sapphire and diamond earrings with matching necklace, and her hair high on her head in a simple style that showed off the depth of her sparkling sky blue eyes, he remembered how excited she'd been when he agreed to share a night out with her only son. He simply didn't have the heart to confess how bone tired he was. "I need a few extra minutes."

Her gaze softened and her hand gently cupped his cheeks. "Hard day?"

"You could say that."

Love and concern shone clearly in her eyes. "What happened?"

He shook his head. "Had to walk Pepper home. She's limping."

"Oh, dear." Her expression crumpled with concern. His mom may not have been cut out to be a country girl, but her kindheartedness extended from animals to humans alike. Tonight's charity du jour was for veterans, next week it could be for stray cats. "Nothing serious, I hope."

"Me too. Randy will let me know, but right now a long hot shower would do me good."

"Take a soak. We can be a little late." She rubbed her hand along his cheek again.

Strangely enough, even though he was a grown man who didn't need or want coddling, his mom's loving touch still had a way of making him feel better. There was no way he could disappoint her by asking to skip tonight. Maybe if he were lucky he could avoid all the annoying people and just spend the night dancing with his mom.

"I'll call for Mary. Have her make you some hot chocolate. Good for the soul after a hard day." Mary had been the family housekeeper since before Jared was born. She was as devoted to the Gold family as she was to her own.

"Thanks, Mom." Offering a return smile and gentle squeeze of her hand, he proceeded up the winding staircase to the master suite at the end of the upstairs hall. He might have to nix the hot chocolate and down a gallon of coffee instead, otherwise his mom might find him sleeping in his soup tonight. Maybe a fifteen minute power nap would help.

Collapsed on his bed, eyes closed, he had no idea if he'd fallen asleep or not when a rap sounded at his bedroom door. "Come in."

The door swung open and carrying a tray, Mary smiled at him sweetly. "Your mother asked me to bring you some hot chocolate. I thought you might prefer coffee. Brought the whole carafe."

"Bless you." He pulled himself upright. There were many things in life he had no doubt about, but he wasn't so sure this house could run without Mary. He knew she was getting up there in years. She'd lost her only son and daughter-in-law in a car accident a few years back and was now raising her only grandson. Some days he thought the responsibility of raising a young boy and taking care of him was more than a woman of her age should take on, and then there were times he was convinced with a heart of gold that woman would outlive them all. At least for tonight, coffee pot in hand, she was his knight in shining armor. Hopefully, for his mother's sake, consumption of the liquid caffeine would be enough to convert him from an exhausted cowboy into Prince Charming.

Read more of Just One Dance available now

MEET CHRIS

Author of dozens of contemporary novels, including the award winning Aloha Series, Chris Keniston lives in suburban Dallas with her husband, two human children, and two canine children. Though she loves her puppies equally, she admits being especially attached to her German Shepherd rescue. After all, even dogs deserve a happily ever after.

More on Chris and her books can be found at www.chriskeniston.com.

Follow Chris on facebook at ChrisKenistonAuthor or on twitter @ckenistonauthor.

Join Chris' newsletter! Enjoy inside peeks and photographs from Chris' world and stories. Some times she'll thank her subscribers with a free copy of a new 99 cent flirt.

Please, if you enjoyed reading Just One Spark, consider helping other readers find The Billionaire Barons of Texas Series by taking a moment to leave a review. Reviews are a blessing to authors and readers alike. Even just a few words will do! Thank you.

Printed in the USA
CPSIA information can be obtained
at www.ICGtesting.com
LVHW051719030424
776262LV00006B/547